A city on fire ignites adventure and passion in two lost souls.

Tyler stepped back as the slats of wood in front of him cracked, as if an earthquake had suddenly split them apart. He watched the crack lengthen, then shielded his eyes as the wall burst apart. Bits of shattered wood flew around him.

When he looked again, he saw a petite, blonde-haired woman holding a black kettle she had used to smash through the wall. Her hair was matted to her head and she was covered in soot and sweat as she stepped through the newly made doorway.

"What are you looking at?" Her voice was husky, dry from the heat. There was a writhing wall of red and yellow behind her. She stepped forward, tottering toward Tyler as if she were drunk. Suddenly she lost consciousness and collapsed into his arms.

I0625991

Fire in Their Hearts

Rita Schulz
And
Russ Crossley

Edited by R. Edgewood

Published by 53rd Street Publishing
Offices in Gibsons, B.C. Canada and Lincoln City, Oregon

Fire in Their Hearts

Published by 53rd Street Publishing
53rd Street Publishing edition Copyright ©2016 Rita Schulz and Russ
Crossley

Cover art © Alanpoulson | Dreamstime.com
Print ISBN 978-1-927621-52-3

Publishing history
Sapphire Blue Publishing 2011
Champagne Books 2013
2016 Edition cover designed by R. Eddewood
Book design and layout © 2016 by 53rd Street Publishing

53rd Street Publishing
Head office: Gibsons B.C. Canada
www.53rdstreetpublishing.com

This is a work of fiction. Any similarities to persons living or dead
are purely coincidental.

Introduction

We are very pleased to bring you this new edition of Fire in Their Hearts. It was co-authored by two of our talented authors many years ago and was first published in 2011 by our good friend, Tina Gerow and her company Sapphire Blue Publishing. For reasons unrelated to the success of her company the rights reverted to the authors and the publishing rights to the book was then granted to Champagne Books who published the book in 2013. What you see now is a revised version proudly published by 53rd Street Publishing.

The book is a historical western romance set in Vancouver, British Columbia in 1886, a banner year for the city. It is the year Vancouver was incorporated and the year the railroad was pushed through to its new terminus in Vancouver. It is also the year half the city burned to the ground. As I said a banner year.

While the story is purely fiction the historical events surrounding the railroad and the fire are not. We hope you will read and enjoy this tale of adventure, danger, and romance on the western edge of civilization in Canada in the 19th century.

To check out more titles by these talented authors see our website http://www.53rdstreetpublishing.com. We publish stories for everyone.

R. Edgewood
Managing Editor
53rd Street Publishing

Prologue

ABNER ROURKE stepped back to admire the wisp of smoke curling from the bottom of the pile of rags and branches piled high in the blackened pit. The fire pit, four feet deep by six feet wide, a hollow in the earth, reminded him of a bowler hat. He had used it many times to dispose of the trash accumulated from clearing the land and building the wooden structures that the city was composed of.

The early morning sun fell hot against Abner's neck. He pulled a dirty handkerchief from his pocket to mop the sweat running down his face. It hadn't rained in four weeks, unusual for Vancouver at this time of year.

A breeze came up. Abner hoped it would help cool him. It carried with it the scent of burning pine needles from the fire, unlike the day a month before when the rains finally ended, and a strong westerly wind had pushed the clouds away from the city and toward the Rocky Mountains that guarded Canada's youngest province from its Eastern neighbors.

The heat of the day and the smoke from the fire made him dizzy, sending him to the pump at the side of the house to splash cold water on his face and head. The fire burned higher with each passing second.

1

Fire in their Hearts

The orange, red, and blue flames danced over the sides of Abner's pit. The wind blew harder, intensifying the flames, pushing them over the lip of the pit toward Abner's wood-framed house.

From the wild grasses to the house itself, the fire was a living creature as it gobbled all in its path and turned the wall into a sheet of flame that crackled as the dry wood caught.

Abner, hearing the sounds of the fire closer than he thought possible, raced to the back door where a wall of heat assailed him. He stepped back and ran through the house, shouting a warning to his wife and children, still asleep in their beds. The family fled to safety with only the clothes on their backs. The flames then leapt to the next house, and the next, carried by the wind, which grew in strength as the blaze worked its way across Vancouver. Residents fled for their lives as they raced to stay ahead of the advancing inferno. Vancouver had no fire department in those days. All was lost.

One

VICTORIA ANN MCNICHOL arrived in Vancouver the day before the fire, June 12, 1886.

Victoria, a blonde-haired, blue-eyed beauty, had a mission. Her father, the Canadian Pacific Railroad boss, Hiram McNichol, was the man who decided which frontier towns died and which survived the westward expansion of Canada's national dream. The railroad would ensure that Canada spread from sea to sea. Someone was trying to kill this dream. Victoria intended to find out who and why.

Prior to leaving Toronto, her father had stressed that something was wrong with the information he was getting about the expansion and the possible terminus of the railroad. There was a lot at stake, and he had to make the correct decision, but he felt he couldn't trust the information. Victoria was here to provide her father with the information he needed, and to find out who was betraying him.

The politicians in Ottawa funded the railroad, which was being constructed by Chinese workers imported to this sparsely populated new world to build a railroad to unite a nation. At the moment, the railroad stopped at New Westminster—the self-titled *Royal City*—to the east of the newly incorporated city of Vancouver.

Fire in their Hearts

Both cities wanted the railroad and, most importantly, the prestige and power that came with it. Both cities had water access, New Westminster had the Fraser River and Vancouver had access on both sides to the Georgia Straight.

To be able to supply her father with the information he needed, Victoria needed to find an updated map of the city and a list of the major real estate owners in Vancouver. She had a list of the owners for Port Moody and New Westminster, the other two cities in competition with Vancouver as the western terminus of the railroad.

Victoria's assumed identity was as a poker player who'd made a personal fortune in the card rooms of Montreal, Toronto, and Boston. She was indeed here to play some of the finest card players the West had to offer. The draw was the first Poker Gathering in Vancouver, organized by the city's founding fathers.

Victoria's education in poker had paid her many benefits in the upscale gambling clubs favored by the elite of polite society in which her mastery of the game was honed. Her father disapproved of her recreational pursuits, but, for now, allowed this indulgence.

Victoria moved onto the wooden boardwalk as the two men who operated the coach service between New Westminster's rail station and Vancouver wrestled her luggage down from the storage box. They grunted as they lifted her large steamer trunk, one at either end, each grasping one of its brass handles. The men carried the trunk, along with her two smaller leather suitcases stacked on top, through the front door of the hotel.

She'd check in to the Tremont House Hotel for two nights until Philip and Constance Walker returned from Toronto. Philip was Canadian Pacific Railroad's man in Vancouver, and had been charged by Hiram with keeping watch over his daughter while she was in the city.

Victoria prepared to step from the coach as the door opened.

"Please allow me," said a smooth, deep voice outside of the coach.

"Thank you," Victoria said as she stepped down onto the boardwalk.

The man standing before her had smiling, warm, dark brown eyes, dark curls that peeked out from beneath a black hat tipped slightly back on his head, and a smile that made her heart flutter. There was a small dimple in his right cheek.

He wore a snow white shirt—Victoria was certain it was silk—with the top button undone, and a gold embroidered vest. A black jacket with matching pants, and polished, black leather boots, completed his dapper outfit. He looked every bit the riverboat gambler.

Victoria's heart skipped a beat as she nodded to him. She took a deep breath, calming herself as she looked at the dry, dusty dirt street outside the Tremont House Hotel and surveyed the scene around her. She looked around as she surreptitiously watched her riverboat gambler walk down the street. Heavily-laden wagons rolled slowly up and down Carrall Street with bales of cloth, bags of flour, crates marked "china," and other goods. The wooden boardwalk kept the foot traffic above the street, a welcome benefit, especially when rain filled it with oozing, stinking mud, which Victoria had heard frequently happened. The boardwalk bustled with women in their floor-length skirts, some with bundles of shopping, others with small children in tow. Although here, she noticed, none wore the high fashion elaborate hats and ringlets common in most eastern communities. In the wilderness of British Columbia, she discovered a world unknown to her.

Fire in their Hearts

These were simple, hard-working people—family people—
and their simple hats and clothing reflected this.

Victoria looked to the north and saw the harbor filled with
ships carrying cargo from the Orient, local fishing boats, and other
smaller vessels sailing, chugging, even being rowed or paddled
across the wide inlet between her and the northern shore. Sawmills
and fish-drying shacks dotted the rocky shoreline.

Prominent against the azure sky stood a range of green and
blue mountains that seemed to cover the horizon. Mighty coastal
peaks stood close, as if guarding this sheltered harbor from all
potential enemies.

Victoria enjoyed playing poker. Her father allowed her to
gamble provided she didn't also take up strong drink. It seemed that
for many of her friends and acquaintances, the two, gambling and
drinking, went together—it had led them to drunken ruin and turned
them into the subject of gossip in the local newspapers.

Victoria agreed with her father on this topic. She had, in
fact, come to loathe alcohol in all its forms, but mostly detested
her fiancé's use of it. Herbert Littlefield, of the Boston Littlefields,
whom she'd met while playing an all-night poker match in Boston,
indulged himself all too frequently, in her opinion. Nonetheless, her
father insisted she marry Herbert to unite their wealthy, powerful
families. The Littlefields owned the largest slaughterhouses in
the Chicago stockyards, while the McNichol's had control of the
railroad. It would be a marriage of industry, not of hearts.

Victoria smiled as she glanced up and down the street, as if
she were a princess surveying her domain, then she followed the
coachmen and entered the Tremont Hotel.

The coachmen dropped the heavy trunk with a thud on the red, blue, and gold Oriental carpet. She thought she could hear their spines crunch and pop, locking into place again as they stood up straight. They wore plain wool pants with jackets and their boots were well worn. They were lean men, hardened by life in this rugged part of the world.

She opened her cloth handbag, extracted two one dollar bills, a very generous tip, and gave them to the leader. At least he'd been the one who'd done all the talking during the five-hour ride over the rough country roads, so she assumed he was the one in charge.

"Thank you, miss," the man said, with a nod of his bald, sweaty head. He glanced at his partner, who shrugged. She knew they worked hard and reached into her handbag again, took out two additional one dollar bills, and handed them to the partner.

"Thank you. Thank you very much, ma'am, ah, miss." He bobbed his head up and down as he gave her a toothy grin. She smiled back at him as he quickly pocketed the money.

Victoria turned toward the large, polished oak desk at the far end of the lobby. A gray-haired woman with wire-rimmed spectacles and a puffy, gray, long-sleeved blouse stood behind the front desk, eyeing her with suspicion, her sharp eyes never leaving Victoria's face as she moved to stand in front of the desk. With a light touch of her hand Victoria felt her elaborate hat to make sure it was in place, gave a little tug to the red-ribbon-threaded black lace falling around its brim, and patted her long blonde ringlets. She smiled briefly, politely, while her cool, dark blue eyes locked on the other woman's as if daring her to make some comment. When she did not, Victoria said, "Hello, I have a reservation. Victoria Kelly. I believe you were expecting me today."

Fire in their Hearts

Victoria waited. The only sound came from a large wooden clock hung on the wall behind the desk. The clock's ornate black hands pointed to the twelve and the four, while the sweeping second hand marched forward to the sound of loud ticks that echoed in the quiet room.

After a moment, the woman smiled, pushing forward a quill standing in an inkwell on one side of the large, leather-bound guest register, which she turned to face Victoria. "Pleased ta meet ya, Miss Kelly. My name is Mrs. Morris. All guests must sign the register upon arrival. Them's the rules." She pointed to the next empty line. "Write your name here." Her tone was surprisingly soft and musical.

Victoria looked down at the empty space in the book. There were five names preceding hers and they were all male. She shrugged—*best not to annoy the natives within minutes of my arrival. That can wait until later.*

She reached for the offered pen and carefully wrote her *nom du plume*, Victoria Kelly, in the empty space. She used the name whenever she went to the card rooms to hide her true identity. Her father's good name must be protected at all costs, should Victoria become either famous—or infamous—in the poker-playing crowd.

Especially on this trip, the city politicians must not know who she was or who her father was. The only ones who knew Victoria's true identity were Philip Walker and his wife.

Even her fiancé, Herbert Littlefield, had not discovered her true identity until it became necessary to form the family alliance. Victoria, of course, swore him to secrecy. Herbert expected her to give up the gaming tables once they married— no decent married woman played cards. Besides, following the wedding, her picture would be all over the society pages of the major eastern dailies.

No, after her marriage, Victoria Kelly, card player of renown, would simply disappear, never to be seen or heard from again. At least she still had some time to enjoy her anonymity. Engagements need not be rushed. Besides, her mission for her father took precedence, at least for the time being.

Victoria regretted her fiancé's attitude about her life as a poker player, but then all good things must end. She sighed inwardly at the thought. She'd miss the excitement of the win. The challenge poker offered was far more than she would have as a wife and mother.

Victoria replaced the quill pen in the inkwell. "Please have someone bring my belongings to my room," she said, accepting the key the woman handed her.

"Where is the nearest card room?" Victoria asked. "I need to warm up my game for the gathering, and where is Water Street?"

She wondered if the woman would attempt to deflect her question with a claim of virtue, but she only glanced up from the register, a momentary flash of unmistakable anger in her eyes. *These stuffy, artificial rules and double standards are enough to drive any intelligent woman mad. One set of rules for men and another for women—ridiculous.*

After that brief look of disgust, the desk clerk settled back to her business-like coolness. "Down Carrall Street two blocks, turn right at the corner, and you'll see the Oriental. That's where the players will be meeting tomorrow, Miss. Kelly, and Water Street is just three blocks north, toward the mountains."

Victoria nodded. *That was relatively easy and painless. Rather nice for a change.* Many women would've called her shameless, or worse, but this woman knew a paying customer when she saw one. *Good for her.*

Fire in their Hearts

She turned and started for the door, feeling the landlady's eyes boring through her back like hot coals. Outside she took a deep breath of the early summer air, smelling faintly of salt and dry timbers. It would still be light for several hours, the summer solstice being a few days away. The longest day of the year meant that, at Vancouver's northerly latitude, the skies would be light until almost ten in the evening.

With her long, loose stride, Victoria started down the boardwalk toward the corner of the street, as instructed by the older woman. She nodded to people she passed. Her cloth handbag, decorated with an intricate stitched design of a bird in flight, swung lightly from her left arm.

The men acknowledged her with a smile, a nod, and a tip of their hats. The women glared at her, keeping their hands folded tightly in front of them, they were proper women, but to Victoria it seemed as if it were to keep her, the oddly-dressed woman, from snatching their handbags.

She'd seen similar reactions many times, and each time she was more amused than the last. If they only knew her true identity they would be shocked, that she was Victoria McNichol of the respectable, prominent Toronto railroad McNichols, and not just a woman gambler named Victoria Kelly.

After the long trip, the warm sunshine and the smell of the dry dirt of the street, mingled with the pleasant scent of the wildflowers and grasses growing along the sides of the buildings, were welcome. Victoria was thankful for the walk. It allowed her time to clear her thoughts before she engaged in battle.

She reached the corner of Carrall and Hastings Streets and spotted the large wooden sign—painted bright red, with "Oriental Hotel" spelled out in ostentatious gold lettering—hanging over the entrance to the two-story, wood-framed building. A spacious wooden walkway ran down the street in front of the structure. Twin saloon-style doors moved constantly with the traffic of men moving in and out of the gambling parlor. Solid doors that could be closed in inclement weather stood open on either side of the swinging western doors, Victoria waited until two lumbering wagons piled high with large wooden kegs of ale passed by then she crossed to stand in front of the Oriental Hotel's twin doors.

She was startled when she heard a man's voice behind her. "This is no place for a lady."

A quick surge of uncontrolled anger rose in her. She'd heard this particular phrase so often she thought she was over getting angry about it. This was a man's world and men expected women to be subservient to their will. But Victoria was a new breed of woman and had other ideas. Things were going to change.

She whirled, ready for a fight, and came face-to-face with the owner of the voice. Her breath caught in her throat. Her riverboat gambler.

The man was beautiful. His eyes were a warm, chocolate brown with flecks of gold. When he tipped his hat, she noticed that his hair was dark, thick and wavy. Then he smiled at her, and the dimple in his cheek made an appearance. When she looked at him her heart constricted in her chest as her knees grew weak. For the first time in her life, Victoria McNichol was at a loss for words.

Victoria lift her chin and smiled at him as she collected her thoughts. She had to stay in character, but she also remembered she wasn't here just to gamble.

That didn't prevent her from feeling a warmth growing in the pit of her stomach.

"Well, why don't we see how the gathering goes? After all, if the men are gentlemen, they shouldn't have any problem with a lady at the table, should they?"

"You are correct, miss, we will see."

Victoria turned from the riverboat gambler as she looked up at the Oriental Hotel. She took a deep breath to calm herself as she entered the wide oak door that he held open for her. She nodded a thank you as she gracefully passed him on the way into the lobby. Her knees felt weak, but she maintained a steady walk and knew that her weakness didn't show, at least she hoped it didn't.

She stopped to look around the lobby. It was done in red and gold with large Oriental vases on either side of the main doors and two that flanked either side of the large dinning room and salon. The gambler nodded to two men who stood by the large oak staircase in the lobby and went to speak with them.

She went to the large carved double oak doors and looking into the salon. The walls were painted a light yellow, a nice contrast to the dark oak floor, and long, red floor length drapes ran along one side of the room. They had a variety of round wooden tables of different sizes, with simple wooden chairs that could be moved, but nothing could be hidden in or under. It was a nice large space with a high ceiling.

Good. She always liked to get the lay of the land and familiarize herself with a venue before she started to play.

As she left she made sure that she didn't look at or for the gambler and made sure that she focused on what she needed to do next and that was to find Mr. H. B. Smith with the Vancouver Water Works.

He had just finished a detailed map of Vancouver, registered at the Land Title Office, and she wanted to get a copy of it.

Victoria walked toward the mountains, making sure that she got her bearings so she could find her way back to the Tremont Hotel. She arrived and found herself in a tall room with a bright window in the front and rows and rows of shoulder-high wooden cabinets. She made her request for the surveyor's map, pleased to find that she could purchase one.

It was a beautiful late afternoon, the sun was warm and there was a light breeze coming from the ocean. She enjoyed her walk back to the hotel and being able to stretch her legs, especially after being on the train and in a coach. She took her time and looked at the large windows, with goods on display and ornate store fronts.

Victoria went back to the Tremont Hotel and unpacked her luggage. It had been a long day of travel, and she was famished and tired. What she needed now was a good meal. Later she would write to Father and tell him she was in Vancouver and ready to conduct her investigation.

With her skirts swishing, her head held high, she strolled along the spacious hallways at the Tremont. The halls were painted a light rose, with framed paintings of old English hunting scenes and countrysides on the walls, which contrasted well against the dark doors. She took her time walking down the wide wooden staircase, enjoying the feel of its smooth, dark, wooden railing under her fingers. She admired the large, oval portraits on the walls in the front lobby as she walked to the front desk.

Looking around the lobby Victoria saw Mrs. Morris, the woman who'd helped her check in, arranging fresh flowers in a glass vase on a side table. Victoria interrupted. "Excuse me."

Mrs. Morris straightened one last stem of bronze chrysanthemum and faced her.

"Yes? How kin I help ya?"

"I'm sorry for bothering you—those are lovely flowers—but could you recommend somewhere I might go for a meal?"

Mrs. Morris smiled at Victoria. "We have a right nice dinin' room just down the hall to yor right. Serves the best roast beef in Vancouver, if I do say so myself."

Victoria liked the woman's enthusiasm. "That sounds like an excellent idea."

***

He'd just left an all-night poker game with some of the more prominent city elders, especially Walter Diller, the principal sponsor of the poker game.

The deep breast pockets of his gambler's jacket were barely able to contain the fresh bills the men had bestowed upon him with regularity through their lack of skills. He made his living gambling, especially poker. He'd tried other games—roulette, faro—but poker was his most profitable game.

It took nerves of steel, plenty of attitude, and as much skill as luck to be successful. The ability to read one's opponent was the most important element in the game. After the first three hands, Tyler recognized all of his opponents' 'tells.' It continually amazed him when people displayed bad habits at the card table. Pulling ears, twitching eyes, changes in breathing—all indicators of the cards each player held. He'd met only a few professional gamblers, like himself, in the card rooms of San Francisco, Seattle, and Portland. Vancouver was new ground—untouched, virgin territory, ripe for the picking.

So far Tyler hadn't seen any known professional players in this town.

If his luck held and they didn't show up, he expected this would be a profitable trip.

English pounds were as good U.S. greenbacks any day. Tyler wasn't so sure, however, about this Dominion of Canada currency the townspeople carried. The 'shinplasters,' as the locals called them, were small paper bills, each worth twenty-five cents. Tyler shook his head at the first player who placed one on the table as an ante, but soon became used to seeing them in the winners' pots, many of which were his. He didn't know if he could even convert the stuff to U.S. cash. But there was a high probability that the currency in his pockets was enough to get him to Canada's eastern provinces, where he could kick the mud of this frontier town from his boots. He'd get to the *real* money in the gentleman's gaming rooms in the east. But he would need both, travel and stake money, and the more the better.

He didn't have a sufficient stake to access those kinds of places yet, but Vancouver would change his fortunes and his future.

It helped that some of the sailors who ventured into the game later in the evening were from U.S. cargo ships anchored in the harbor, and had the courtesy to leave behind some of their U.S. currency.

Tyler looked out his third floor window toward the south, and saw orange flames topped with grey billowing smoke engulf buildings on the edge of the city five or six blocks away.

He continued to watch as another building caught on fire. It seemed to be getting closer and heading toward his hotel. He gathered up his winnings and turned to the door. He had to alert everyone a raging fire was heading toward them.

Two

VICTORIA AWOKE, opening her eyes with a start. She'd seen the dark stranger in her dreams, the one with whom she had crossed paths twice yesterday. She didn't know the man's name yet. *Who was he? Where did he come from?*

She knew it was improper for an engaged woman to think about another man. She pushed the thoughts deeper inside her mind, trying to get comfortable. Her hair and body were sticky with perspiration. She threw back the bed covers in an attempt to cool down.

A frantic knocking on her door made her sit up, as a woman's voice calling her name urged her to come to the door.

It took Victoria a moment to recognize the voice. *Mrs. Morris. The landlady.*

She heard the sharp edge of fear in Mrs. Morris' voice. The resonance sent a shiver through her. Suddenly Victoria was fully alert. She gathered the folds of her nightgown in her hands and ran to the door, her bare feet surprisingly warm in the early morning air.

The din coming from outside her door sounded like a cattle stampede. The sound of running feet thumped down the hallway. Victoria opened the door a crack to see Mrs. Morris' flushed face.

Her raised right hand was clenched in a fist ready to pound on the door again.

Victoria swung the door open wide, her expression puzzled. "What is it?"

"Wildfire! It's reached the town and is close to the hotel," said the older woman. Her long gray hair was pulled back into an untidy braid. Her panicked eyes flitted down the corridor as she quickly shuffled down the hall to the next door. Victoria saw other guests, still in their nightclothes, running with half-open suitcases for the stairs.

Victoria's eyes widened. *What should I take?* she thought frantically. Her eyes darted back and forth. *How long do I have?*

Victoria scanned her room, reaching for the leather money belt she usually wore under the folds of her skirts. It now contained her stake for the gathering—twenty thousand dollars. More money than most people would see in their lifetimes.

She briskly moved to the bed and, with trembling fingers, wrapped the belt about her waist. Next, she moved to the closet and pulled out her leather riding boots.

She knew she had to hurry, but she felt sluggish.

Victoria knew that time was running out and that she had to rouse herself immediately. From the chest of drawers she grabbed a cotton skirt and blouse and dressed quickly. By the time she was finished, the sounds of running feet had subsided from the hallway. Now she heard voices coming from outside her window.

She raced to the window overlooking the street and opened it expecting to see blue sky like the day before. Instead, she saw a wall of flame and black smoke moving toward the hotel. Flames leapt from building to building. The smoke was thick and harsh as it invaded her nose, mouth, and throat.

Fire in their Hearts

She coughed and her eyes teared up. The soot clung to her tongue. When she tried to swallow, its bitterness burned her throat.

The fire moved quickly, as if it were a living thing that hoped to consume as much as possible. It seemed as if the whole world were burning and about to be consumed in the fires of hell. The roar of the flames deafened as it consumed building after building. The inferno was feeding its insatiable hunger.

Victoria rushed out to the hall and ran down to the stairs leading to the lobby, the smoke billowing around her, getting thicker by the minute.

Am I too late to get out?

Victoria moved toward the front entrance only to find it blocked by a wall of yellow and orange flames. She shielded her face from the intense heat with her arms, and made her way around the bottom of the staircase to the dining room. From the dining room she ran into the kitchen, where she expected to find a way out.

The kitchen was deserted—and the only door was on a wall already on fire. Victoria was trapped. Terrified, her heart beat hard against her chest. She started at the loud crackle of burning wood as the kitchen door behind her caught on fire. She saw flames lick their way up the inside walls. The fire was coming for her and had blocked her escape. She swallowed hard and looked around, there had to be something she could do. There had to be a way out.

***

Walter Diller suddenly burst through the door into Tyler's room. The sweat on his saggy jowls reflected in his wild eyes.

"Miss Kelly's trapped at the Tremont," Diller said, gasping for breath. He stopped to pull a soiled handkerchief from the pocket of his shirt.

Tyler easily recalled the blonde, blue-eyed beauty and the way she made his breath catch in his chest.

She was in trouble, and he knew from the men he'd been gambling with that this town didn't yet have a fire department or any equipment to stop the blaze, let alone rescue someone.

He didn't know what he would do exactly, but that young woman wasn't about to die in this fire.

Three

TYLER RACED THROUGH the burning streets of Vancouver gripping an axe firmly, his shoulders square and his stride loose. He marched between the burning buildings, making his way toward the Tremont Hotel. His face gleamed with sweat and the dark curls that normally fell across his tanned forehead were pasted to his scalp. Tyler's breathing was labored from the heat and lack of oxygen. He'd removed his jacket and vest, and his soaked shirt was unbuttoned. Overhead clouds of acrid, black smoke had turned the morning into night.

Tyler cursed softly as he found the way ahead blocked by a wall of flame that leapt in the air some twenty feet above his head. He turned to his right and quickly made his way down a side street until he was able to see the Tremont. From where he stood it seemed as if it was engulfed in flames, except for the rear wall. Smoke seeped from cracks in the tortured wood, while the heat caused the wall to undulate as if it were alive.

I only have one chance at this.

He would need to cut his way through the rear wall and hope he guessed correctly. From what he'd seen, Miss Kelly, with her intelligent blue eyes and bright determined smile, appeared to be a very astute woman. He expected her to be nearest the rear wall of the hotel where the fire was less intense. If she had any hope of rescue or escape, it would be from there.

Tyler walked along the wall until he found what seemed to be the coolest spot. He hefted the axe over his shoulder, took a deep breath, readied himself to strike a blow, then hesitated when he heard a loud rending of wood audible even over the roar of the hungry fire.

He stepped back as the slats of wood in front of him cracked, as if an earthquake had suddenly split them apart. He watched the crack lengthen, then shielded his eyes as the wall burst apart. Bits of shattered wood flew around him.

When he looked again, he saw a petite, blonde-haired woman holding a black kettle she had used to smash through the wall. Her hair was matted to her head and she was covered in soot and sweat as she stepped through the newly made doorway.

"What are you looking at?" Her voice was husky, dry from the heat. There was a writhing wall of red and yellow behind her. She stepped forward, tottering toward Tyler as if she were drunk. Suddenly she lost consciousness and collapsed into his arms.

The kettle in her hands dropped, sounding like a gong as it fell to her feet and rolled off to the right. He gaped at the woman he held in his arms. In spite of the heat and smoke in the burning building, Miss Kelly had managed to use the huge pot to batter a hole through the wall and escape into the alley. She was truly amazing.

He lifted her easily, lay her across his broad shoulders, and searched for a gap in the wall of flames, which was growing in intensity. He saw a small opening between the buildings that was quickly closing as the flames ravaged the Tremont Hotel. He only had seconds for them to escape.

With a burst of speed, he raced ahead of the flames, managing to get through just as the circle of fire closed off the escape route.

Fire in their Hearts

Once through the gap, Tyler looked back and saw that the entire route he'd just taken was now cut off. The waterfront docks were the only way left open to them. He raced toward the ocean, not knowing if they would survive.

He ran onto a dock extending far into the bay. Here they would be safe from the fire—at least for the moment. He lay Miss Kelly on her side then scanned the harbor for something that would float.

But the buildings near the dock were quickly disappearing in the blaze. Tyler heard timbers crashing as the inferno consumed the part of the dock nearest to the shore, burning their only escape route. It wouldn't be long before they were forced to the very end of the dock. They would soon be in the water. Drowning or burning seemed to be their only choices.

He didn't know how to swim and Miss Kelly had not yet revived. If she could swim at least she would be able to save herself. He gazed at her delicate features, even though he didn't know much about her, at least he would die in the presence of true beauty.

The dock swayed beneath them as the supporting beams burned and it became unstable. It swayed more violently to the right, then seemed to stop as if suspended by a thread.

He heard a rough cough then glanced down at the woman, whose eyes were blinking open. She rolled to one side, moaned, and coughed hard to clear her lungs.

She sat up. "Where am I?" she gasped in a hoarse whisper. She blinked furiously, tears running down her cheeks in dirty rivulets.

"We're at the end of a dock—trapped by the fire," Tyler said grimly.

She wiped her face with her grimy hands and looked at him, her brow furrowed. "Who are you?"

"Tyler Scott, ma'am." He reached up to instinctively tip a non-existent hat, then shrugged and nodded toward the flames at the end of the dock.

She glanced at the orange and yellow flames, frowned, and sat up straight. "Well, why don't we swim?"

Tyler shrugged and grinned at her. "I don't swim," he said, as if it were obvious.

"You men." Victoria shook her head as she rose to her feet. Standing next to Tyler on the precariously listing dock, she looked around to get her bearings. "Well, I do."

With that, she grabbed him by one arm, pulled him to the end of the dock, and pushed him into the water. She took a deep breath then leapt in herself.

He felt himself sink into the dark, soot-stained water, going deep into its murky depths. His vision blurred so he closed his eyes, expecting this was the end. Then two slender arms wrapped around his chest, pulled, and lifted him toward the surface. He went limp, fully expecting this was Gabriel the archangel come to take him to the pearly gates.

Instead, he sputtered as he burst to the surface of the bay, spitting out the saltwater in his mouth. One of Victoria's arms wrapped about under his chin, supporting his head. He could feel her soft body with its more than ample curves press against his back.

"Don't panic and we'll get through this. Try to relax." Victoria's voice was firm and close to his ear.

Kicking hard, she swam toward a rocky beach across the bay. It looked to Tyler to be a long way to swim.

Not that he was any judge of distance in the water since he'd never actually been swimming before. Within ten minutes, they'd made their way out of the water to the seaweed- and barnacle-covered rocks on the beach.

The sharp barnacles cut their hands as they climbed the rocks to the grass at the top of a short rise above the high tide line. Finally, he and Victoria lay side by side on their backs, coughing and breathing hard as they cleared their lungs from the smoke and water.

"This feels good," Victoria said, taking in large gulps of air. The fresh scent of pine and oak trees that surrounded them helped clear their lungs from the smoke.

They turned simultaneously and gazed into each other's eyes, giggling like children when they saw their faces were streaked with black from the dirty, soot-filled water.

Victoria's expression suddenly changed to a frown and her eyes narrowed.

Tyler's brow furrowed, too. He was puzzled. "What?" he said gently, forcing his hands to stay at his sides even though he desperately wanted to reach out and hug his rescuer.

"You were coming to rescue me, weren't you?"

He nodded.

"Why?" she asked as she sat down on a large clump of grass within arms' length of him.

He shrugged. "It seemed the right thing to do at the time."

"You don't know me, do you?"

"Should I?"

"No. We've never met before yesterday that I remember. So you risked your life to save a stranger?"

***

Victoria rose to her feet, looked down, and studied her clearly ruined clothing. She knew everything else she owned would have been destroyed in her hotel room.

She ran a hand around her waist and was relieved to find the money belt still intact beneath her shirt. The bills were wet, but they'd eventually dry. What she needed right now was a place to change out of her wet clothes and to spread the money out to dry. *I know that the Walkers won't be back until tomorrow, so where can I go?*

"Problem?" asked Tyler.

Victoria glanced at him, then her expression softened when she gazed into his eyes, which drew her in like magnets. Tyler smiled. The sight of the dimple in his right cheek made a twinge of pleasure travel through her. The grime seemed to amplify his handsomeness. His shirt, open to his waist, revealed strong, wide shoulders, a chest with dark, curly hair, and a rippling stomach Victoria was certain was tough enough to scrub her laundry on.

She smiled slightly. "Sorry. Mr. Scott, is it? Where are you from?"

He nodded casually. "I'm from south of the border and you can call me Ty, Miss Victoria, everyone else does."

She experienced a flash of anger at his presumption of familiarity, then pushed it aside. The man was her knight in shining armor, after all, and he was handsome beyond words, but she didn't appreciate his cockiness in using her Christian name. Just because he was extremely good-looking and had saved her life didn't entitle him to special treatment.

Not from me, Mr. Tyler Scott.

"Listen, Mr. Scott," she began, ignoring his request to use his Christian name. After all, they hadn't been properly introduced. Just because they were half-naked—him with his shirt half off and her with her wet clothing clinging to her like her own skin—didn't mean they should abandon the need for social graces and formal introductions. They were civilized people, after all, not some heathens.

"Until such time as we are properly introduced, I would prefer to use your family name. And I would appreciate your using mine as well. Miss Victoria Kelly."

His eyes shone with a mixture of amusement and guile. Before he could reply, a buckboard wagon rattled and lurched nosily toward them, drawn by two large horses. On board the wagon, Victoria saw two men she didn't recognize. One man was holding his wide-brimmed skimmer in place with one hand while he gripped the reins of the horses with the other as they bounced along the pot-holed trail.

The second man was extremely slender, dressed in a dark suit buttoned all the way to his skinny neck. He wore wire-rimmed spectacles and his pale face was fixed in a grim expression that reminded Victoria of a weasel.

A breeze came up and Victoria shivered. She knew that she would have to get out of her wet clothing quickly or risk getting a chill.

The wagon came to a stop near them. The driver's eyes went wide and the thin man gasped and averted his eyes upon seeing Tyler and Victoria close together lying on the grass.

The two horses snorted uneasily. Victoria frowned at the wagon's occupants as the driver tossed her a thick wool blanket from inside the wagon.

She draped it around her shoulders then pulled it tight when she saw his leering stare. She felt naked and angry. She glared at him as she wrapped the blanket even closer around her shoulders.

"Gentlemen," she nodded, her eyes remaining on the driver, who was staring at her. She met his eyes, refusing to look away. He finally averted his gaze with a slight shrug of his broad shoulders.

"We're so glad the two of you are safe," said portly Mayor Diller. He handed the reins to the thin man and clambered down from the wagon's bench seat. The thin man remained seated, his lips pursed in a grim line.

"Thank you, Mayor." Tyler grinned. "We, too, are pleased with the situation. Miss Kelly and I are both uninjured."

Victoria looked toward the flames. The dark skeletal remains of the buildings that made up the core of the city stood across the bay from them. The blackened wood reminded Victoria of headstones, commemorating the death of the newly incorporated city. Vancouver had barely begun, and now it was gone. Victoria sighed. "I suppose I may as well move to New Westminster if the hotels are either destroyed or full. I guess that means that the gathering will be cancelled?"

The mayor looked horrified, his jaw loose and his eyes wide. "No, please, miss, there's no need for that. The gathering…"

"…is cancelled." Tyler's voice betrayed his disappointment.

The mayor, interestingly, stayed silent, but Victoria noticed an odd little twitch at the corner of his eyes. She knew well the look of someone with a card up his sleeve. For the moment she would keep her opinion to herself. No point in letting her competition know she was adept at reading people or opponents. It was noteworthy, too, that Tyler seemed to have missed the cue from Mayor Diller. *A good sign.*

"How many lives lost?" asked Tyler.

"Hopefully none," said the thin man, "thank the Lord."

The man's comment elicited a small grimace from Mayor Diller, who turned slightly to face the thin, severe-looking man. "Let me introduce you, I'm Mayor Diller and this is Reverend Sloan, our local man of God."

Sloan nodded toward the men.

They nodded in kind, eyeing each other like wary animals.

Victoria relaxed a little, understanding now Reverend Sloan's tension over her clothing, or lack thereof. Still, she could barely contain her feeling of insult at the larger man's lewd stare. After all, she'd been snatched from the jaws of death only moments before. It was not as if she were some harlot. In her opinion, even if she were as naked as the day she was born, it would be proper in the circumstances..

"Shall we?" said Diller, who climbed onto the wagon, his wide posterior sticking out behind him. With a grunt, he reseated himself on the bench seat next to the reverend.

"Miss Kelly." Tyler bowed and waved his hand to allow her to pass to the rear of the wagon. He kept his sparkling dark eyes, and a wry grin, fixed on her.

Tyler opened the wooden gate at the rear of the wagon's flat wooden deck and offered a hand to assist her. Victoria grasped his warm hand in hers and climbed up to sit on the seat. Then she watched as Tyler climbed aboard easily to sit beside her.

The skies were slowly clearing of smoke. As the wagon bumped its way along the rock-strewn trail, a flock of geese lifted off from the beach where they'd sat as silent observers to the human tragedy unfolding across the shallow bay.

Rita Schulz and Russ Crossley

The sky to the east was a hazy orange and red from the afternoon sunlight struggling to cut through the soot. The fire, having burned what it could, left the charred ruin of the city in its wake like some infernal tidal wave. The city's eleven thousand souls faced a considerable challenge to get Vancouver back to some sense of order.

Four

VICTORIA WATCHED AS Mayor Diller glanced around at the ruined city without emotion and twisted the dark mustache that curved like a pigeon's wing over his upper lip. His mouth was a tight line.

As they drove into town, she saw Mr. Smart strolling down the street toward them. The mayor quickly jumped to the ground, then rounded the horses to slap Smart on his broad back with a whoop of joy. "Mr. Smart, my good man, how fortunate for you that your land was recently cleared. Your fine palace survived this morning's unfortunate events."

Hank Smart, a new resident and owner of Vancouver's recently completed Brighton Hotel, looked at the mayor, confusion etched in his furrowed brow.

The mayor is the perfect politician, quick to heap praise and very likely to take credit in the next breath. Victoria chuckled.

Dazed citizens were returning to the center of the city to dig out whatever they could salvage. The townsfolk wore angry expressions as they saw the mayor standing with his arm over Hank Smart's shoulder wearing his best *I-want-your-vote* smile. They didn't need him to play the politician, right now they needed help.

The mayor looked down the street at the crowd of angry people headed in their direction.

As with all politicians, he was never one to pass up a speaking opportunity, and as the crowd drew near he launched into an ill-prepared speech designed to allay their fears.

Victoria cast a glance at Tyler, who smirked and returned her look with an easy grin. *How could I be so foolish? I've let my guard down in front of this perfect stranger. I know better than that.* He'd been far too familiar, especially for someone she'd just met.

"Citizens of Vancouver, Mr. Harold…"

"It's Hank," interrupted Hank.

Diller glared at Hank. His feigned smile disappeared, but quickly returned.

"As I was saying, Mr. *Hank* Smart is about to open his newly built hotel to the citizens of Vancouver to serve your needs. It is in times of crisis like this that good citizens, such as my good friend Hank here—"

"I never—"

Ignoring the hotel owner's protests, Diller continued, undeterred. "—such as Hank come to the aid of our community. Mr. Smart and I will confer inside, but very soon the doors will open and we will commence plans to rebuild the city. And we'll proceed with the first annual world championship poker gathering, right here in our fair city at this hotel after only a short delay of a week."

People around them nodded and looked pleased at the prospect of hosting the poker gather. Tyler had a slight smile on his face and seemed more relaxed. *Perhaps this poker gather is really important to him. Something to keep in mind.*

With that, Victoria watched, amused, as Diller and Smart walked up the three wooden steps to disappear inside the front door of the hotel. The glass in the door rattled loudly as they closed it behind them.

Fire in their Hearts

The breeze was strong now, kicking up ashes and fanning dying embers, wood smoke was still thick in the air. Tyler, Victoria, and the crowd stood and watched the two men argue through the glass door. They stood in the lobby by the check-in desk, their arms waved and their fists pounded on the desk in an animated discussion, no doubt filled with language so colorful it would turn the air blue.

A bird flitted by overhead and called to its companions.

Victoria watched first one, then another of the small, red-breasted birds fly playfully overhead. It occurred to her how the world went on even in the face of a cataclysm. She sighed at the irony.

Out of the corner of her eye, she saw Tyler frown and his forehead wrinkle. His dark eyebrows arched.

"Everything all right, Miss Kelly?"

She nodded, averting her gaze from his. She didn't want to look into his eyes, afraid she would be lost in them. The man was a threat every time she looked at him. *He is so good looking, and I'm an engaged woman with a mission to fulfill. I have no time for distractions.*

The door to the hotel finally opened, and Smart emerged followed by a red-faced Mayor Diller. Hank looked sheepish, yet the twinkle in his eyes indicated to Victoria that he'd won the argument.

"Come in.," Smart said, looking at Tyler and Victoria, then stood to one side. The crowd murmured its displeasure at not being included, then dispersed to begin the work of rebuilding their lives.

As the mayor continued to stand in the street, waving the crowd away, rocking back and forth on his heels, and smiling broadly at anyone who gave him a disparaging look, Hank Smart led Victoria and Tyler inside the hotel, closing the door behind them.

The lobby of the hotel was surprisingly plush. The front reception desk was constructed of highly polished cedar, a fine Oriental rug covered the wood floor. In front of the large picture window sat an ornately carved lounger and a small cedar table. The oil lamp on the table had a clear glass cover and a base painted with angels in flight. It reminded Victoria of those paintings she'd seen in the museums in Europe where her father had once taken her.

A grandfather clock stood watch in the corner, the ticking of its mechanism being the only sound that interrupted the silence of the room, which was filled with warmth and charm.

"I've got two rooms already made up, if you want to get yourselves cleaned up," said Smart. "My wife, Em, will bring you hot water for the bath. There is only one bath, I'm afraid—at the end of the hall upstairs." He glanced inquiringly at Tyler, who grinned.

"Then I guess we'll have to share." The handsome gambler winked at Victoria.

Victoria's face grew warm as she looked away. *How rude. How dare he suggest such a thing!* Even though she'd had the exact thought cross her mind at the same time. *We still haven't even been formally introduced.* She had been taught that manners were a priority for a lady and of the utmost importance.

"Oh, excuse me," added Tyler. "I knew I'd forgotten something. Mr. Smart, would you please formally introduce me to Miss Kelly?"

Smart looked confused. "I thought—"

Tyler smiled. "Unfortunately, no. We've only just met—when we saved each other's lives."

"Huh...I guess..." "Miss Kelly, please help me here."

"Certainly, Mr. Smart. My name is Victoria Kelly of the Toronto Kelly's. I am here to play in the poker gathering."

"I'm Tyler Scott of the Boston Scott's," said Tyler. "and I'm here for the poker gathering, as well. It's a real pleasure to finally meet you, Miss Kelly, after all we've been though together."

Tyler grinned at Victoria, winked at her, then bowed deep at the waist, his flippant attitude more than obvious.

"I have no intention of consorting with this," she said, casting a glance at Tyler, "*gentleman.*"

Victoria spun away and started for the stairs. Smart rushed behind the desk and retrieved the two room keys.

"Em!" he called as he followed Victoria.

They heard a woman's voice call from the floor above. "Yes, Hank?"

"Em, we have two guests checking in."

"We're not ready yet." A woman wearing a lavender dress with a white apron appeared at the top of the stairs. She checked herself as she saw the red, soot-covered faces and wet clothes of the two guests. "Oh, my." was all she said as she started down the stairs.

Her blonde hair was pulled into a large bun atop her head, which looked even larger since she had a long, narrow face. Her intense brown eyes surveyed the two strangers. She broke into an easy grin. "Sorry, folks," she said brightly, "I see you two need a place to clean up as soon as possible. Hank's done the right thing."

Victoria felt an instant liking for this strong frontier woman. "I'm Victoria Kelly."

"This must be the mister?" said Emily Smart, nodding to Tyler.

Victoria felt her palms get damp as she shook her head. Her cheeks burned. "Oh, no. Most certainly not."

34

After getting the keys from her husband and without asking anything further Emily led Tyler and Victoria upstairs while Hank returned back to the lobby.

"We have a bar in the back, so I better hurry and get it open it for the no doubt thirsty patrons whose watering holes disappeared this morning," he explained as he left them.

***

Upstairs Emily unlocked the doors to their rooms and promised to return with clean, dry clothes for each of them. "I'll let you know when the bath is drawn, Miss Kelly." she said, casting a disparaging glance at Tyler. "And you, sir, will go second. And alone." She smiled and eyed him knowingly.

Tyler grinned in amusement as he stepped into his room, closing his door behind him.

Victoria thanked Emily and entered her room, holding the large towel Emily had given her carefully away from her soot-covered body. *I doubt the clothes will fit well, but they'll do for now. It's very sweet of Emily to offer them.*

After Emily left, Victoria studied the room. A metal-framed bed sat against one wall, covered by a beige quilt. Brown throw rugs covered the hardwood floor. A small end table, made of a dark stained wood, sat next to the bed with a matching mirrored dresser opposite it. A window overlooked the street in front of the hotel. Floor-length curtains were open to let the sunlight stream through. This was much nicer than her room at the Tremont Hotel.

Victoria moved to the dresser and untucked her shirt to reveal her money belt. She took off the shirt first, then undid the leather belt, which was cutting into her waist and leaving behind an angry red mark. The leather had shrunk as it dried, causing it to become tighter against her body.

She sighed with relief as she removed the belt and rubbed her tortured belly and sides. Her normally smooth, white skin felt rough to her touch as she fingered the red welts caused by the damp leather.

She undid the strings that held the belt closed and pulled out the money. There were denominations of five, ten, and twenty dollar bills. She separated them by denomination then laid each bill carefully atop the length of the dresser. She hoped they'd dry quickly. If the poker gathering proceeded as planned, she'd need a dry stake.

She hadn't appreciated the look in Tyler Scott's eye or his comment earlier when she revealed she was a gambler and that she intended to be at the gathering. Men had very little respect for women who played poker even if they did as well as or better than they did.

She'd seen the look before. She was certain Tyler was one of those men who thought women should be at home—barefoot and pregnant.

She was determined to be at the gathering. She'd show him, and every other man at the table, that she was a match for them. She was more than capable of holding her own at any card table, no matter what the stakes or who the players.

There was a light knock on the door. Mrs. Smart had returned.

Victoria wrapped the towel around her naked body, went to the door, and opened it. Then slammed it shut when she realized who stood in the hallway. *Tyler Scott!*

"Miss Kelly, may I speak with you for a moment?" He hesitated. "I wish to apologize for my bad manners earlier."

She considered his request for a second, then threw the door open again. *Nudity be hanged.*

"I know what you're doing," she said, her tone even and forceful, startling him into silence. "It's an old gambler's trick. Unnerve your opponent by being overly polite. Well know this, *Mr. Tyler Scott*. I've played in the finest card rooms in the east and no tricks will help you at the table."

She slammed the door in his face before he could utter a word. *I showed him.* She was pleased with herself. She let the towel loosen as she turned back to look at her bank notes.

There was another knock on the door. "Please leave me alone," she called though the closed door.

"It's Mrs. Smart, with dry clothes."

Victoria silently cursed herself, then, after wrapping the towel snugly again around her body, she pulled the door open. "I'm so sorry, Mrs. Smart...it's just that—"

"I understand, dear. I was on the stairs. I heard the exchange between you and Mr. Scott. Oh, and please call me Em. Everyone does."

Victoria looked at Em, she liked the woman, but she felt it prudent that no one knew how much money she had with her.

Victoria quickly thanked Em as she carefully took the stack of dry clothes from her. Victoria made sure that her towel didn't come loose as she put everything on the bed and looked at the clothes—a light blue skirt with a bustle, a plain white cotton blouse, underclothes, and a simple hat.

Victoria sighed. She usually wore expensive hats, her hair done up in ringlets and her dresses the latest fashion when she went to poker gatherings. She had found that such a get-up distracted as well as disarmed the men, who thought they were playing against a lady. This tactic had at times tipped the scales in her favor.

The rest of the time, much to her father's chagrin, she preferred to wear simple, straight split skirts without a bustle.

Her father frequently scolded her by asking her how she expected to snare a good man dressing as she did. Her father was loath to admit that his daughter's beauty was a lure that attracted many big fish to her pond. Her recent engagement had silenced that argument, she had and would continue to do her duty.

Herbert Littlefield was a braggart and a rather dull man, but his funds and station would allow Victoria to travel in the cream of society. More importantly, their families would mutually benefit— the children from this union would secure the future of both families. It was more of a corporate merger than a marriage.

Her heart felt heavy at the thought, her eyes filled with tears. She knew it wouldn't be easy, but she planned to make the best of her marriage, perhaps with time she would learn to love Herbert.

There was another knock on the door. *This place is as busy as a train station. It must be Mrs. Smart, Em, again.* Victoria asked who it was, when Em answered, she opened the door.

"The bath is ready at the end of the hall, and there is a lock on the door to maintain a lady's privacy." Em added, "Let me know when you're done so I can let Mr. Scott know it's his turn."

"There's no need, Em. I'll take care of Mr. Scott."

"As you wish." Em shrugged and left Victoria alone. Victoria waited for a few minutes to make sure that Em had gone. Lacking a robe, she took a blanket from the bed and drew it around her, then she gathered the few clothes she had been given. She quietly opened her door, looked intently up and down the hallway to make sure no one was there. She took a deep breath, quickly entered the hallway, and closed her hotel room door behind her.

"Ah, just the person I wanted to see." Tyler casually leaned against the doorway of his room. "As I was saying, I wanted to apologize."

How did he do that? I just checked and there was no one there a second ago, and now here he is. How does he move so fast?

Tyler gazed at her near-naked form, the blanket doing little to hide her firm curves. A sly grin crossed his dark features as a glint like that of a mischievous child appeared in his eyes.

Victoria attempted—but ultimately failed—to keep her expression in check. A slight smile crossed her lips, she looked down at the floor, her eyes narrowed with embarrassment mixed with excitement.

"Mr. Scott." She looked up at him, nodded ever so slightly as her eyes focused on the handsome face before her. Her bright blue eyes met his warm brown ones.

In response, he reached for, then lifted, her left hand to his lips and kissed it softly as if she were a countess. The movement made the blanket slip off her left shoulder, to reveal the bare white skin beneath as well as the slope of her slender neck.

"Miss Kelly, I would be honored if you would bathe first." He released her hand. She let it fall to her side, making no effort to cover her bare shoulder. Her knees weakened as if they were made of Indian rubber, fresh from the subcontinent. Her face grew warm as blood rushed to her cheeks. She felt the urge to invite him to join her in the bath, then pushed it from her mind.

What am I thinking? I'm engaged! Tyler Scott casually turned away from her and strode toward his room. It was too close to the bathing room. Tyler, with a small swagger in his steps, disappeared behind his door and closed it behind himself with a thump.

He smells like licorice.

Fire in their Hearts

Victoria opened, stepped in, and quickly closed her door. Then leaned back against it, fanning her overheated face. She looked at the mirror on the dresser—her face was crimson, flushed from her encounter with Tyler Scott, he certainly was a handsome man.

She waited until her heartbeat returned to normal, then opened the door. After checking to see if the passageway was empty, she headed toward the bathing room, grasping the blanket in an iron grip about her shoulders.

She closed the bathing room door behind her and took a deep breath. She realized she had been holding her breath fearing someone—in particular a Mr. Tyler Scott—might hear her. The thin walls of the building probably announced her arrival anyway, but she didn't need any additional advertisement of her movements. She let out a soft breath then quietly took another.

She made sure the door was locked, then padded to the armless chair beside the steaming tub of water.

The windowless room had plain, wood-paneled walls and a painting of a country scene hanging over the claw-footed bathtub. The tub was filled halfway with soapy hot water that permeated the air with steam, rising like a heavenly fog. No bath in the world had ever smelled so good to her.

Victoria dropped the rough blanket on a chair and savored the scent of the soap and water. After dipping one toe in first to test the water temperature—which was perfect—she slipped the rest of her body into the hot water. The water was certain to chase away any cold that was left after her swim in the bay.

She completely submerged her body. She floated to the head of the tub until she was able to rest her back on the sloping wall of shining porcelain. She sighed as the warm water enveloped her.

The cold that had permeated her body since she'd swum began to dissipate. She melted away as if she were the polar ice cap in mid-summer.

Victoria closed her eyes and leaned her head back, sinking in the tub until the water came to just below her chin. She was tired and feared she might fall asleep, slip beneath the water, and drown. *The ultimate irony—survive a raging fire, swim across a cold bay, only to perish in one's bath.* She chuckled softly at the irony. Suddenly she bolted upright as she heard a soft knock, then a key being slipped into the lock in the door.

Her heart leapt into her throat. *Is Tyler the kind of man who takes advantage of women?*

The lock released with an audible click in the quiet room. She thought about trying to stop whoever was about to enter by leaping out of the tub, grabbing the towel, and confronting him. Before she could move, the door opened. She ducked her head under the water in a vain attempt to hide her nakedness.

She heard a muffled voice call her name.

Victoria burst through the surface of the water, sputtering until she sat in the middle of the tub. She spat soapy water from her mouth, then blinked hard until her vision cleared. She saw a surprised Emily Smart holding two white towels folded neatly in her arms.

Emily stood frozen in the doorway gaping at the nude woman sitting in the bath. Victoria's round breasts dripped with water and her chest heaved as she gasped for breath.

"Is there a problem, Miss Kelly?"

Victoria smiled weakly and crossed her arms across her chest. "I thought you might be someone else."

41

Fire in their Hearts

Emily slowly nodded and closed the door behind her, as she moved to place the towels on the chair next to the tub. "Don't be startling me like that. Did you think I was that Scott fella? Well, you'd be wrong. No man is gonna take advantage of a young lady's virtue under this roof. I'll have none of those shenanigans on my watch. I run a moral establishment. Not some house of ill repute, like some of the less virtuous joints in this city."

Victoria listened as the older woman prattled on about the lack of morals among the city's elite. Of course, she knew the elite of Vancouver mostly consisted of robber barons, drunks, gamblers, and— of course— the ladies of the city. Unlike the well-bred families of the prosperous East, Vancouver's gentlemen were less than gentle.

Ruthless businessmen and former rascals of every sort had raped the resources from this virgin land, many becoming millionaires overnight. At least the men with their skins still intact after attempts to swindle what they thought were eastern city types.

What they failed to recognize was wealthy men of the East attained their wealth by being equally, if not more, ruthless. The hangman's rope had seen many a confidence man swinging beneath tall eastern oaks and elms.

There were also God-fearing men and women, honest hard-working people who provided labor to build the cities and towns of the new West. The exploits of their rough-and-ready neighbors to the south in the United States were legendary here. Some people feared that such raucous behavior might spill over the border. That law abiding population didn't appreciate the attitude prevalent in the Wild West.

This didn't mean that Victoria's virtue was safe in this outback of civilization.

But she knew, under the watchful eye of her generous host, she would have a modicum of protection from the lustful men Tyler Scott represented. She felt a twinge of regret, maybe he was an exception. She immediately dismissed the idea of any other feeling but loathing for this American card sharp.

"Thank you, Em. I'm sorry if I startled you. I'm most grateful that you took me in after the dreadful events of this morning."

Emily Smart smiled. "Don't be concerned, miss. Hank and I are pleased ta have ya." Emily turned away, walked out, and Victoria heard the soft click of the door being locked.

Victoria sighed forlornly, sank back into the tub, resting her bare back against the wall of enameled porcelain trying to erase Tyler from her mind. She closed her eyes.

"Maybe it wouldn't have been so bad if it had been him," she murmured, thinking of Tyler's handsome features.

Five

TYLER SCOTT LOOKED into his dresser mirror as he rubbed his stubbled chin and realized he hadn't shaved since yesterday. What would a woman with the obvious class of Victoria Kelly think of a scruffy, unshaven American gambler?

She was beautiful beyond belief, the moment he laid eyes on her slender, lithe form as he helped her down from the stage coach he had felt drawn to her. Especially when her wet cotton shirt and skirt stuck to her as if they were painted on, leaving very little to the imagination. Her sassy, confident manner, and wide, sapphire blue eyes attracted him even more.

He hoped the encounter in the hotel hallway and the glimpse of her shoulder was a forbearer of more to come. He wanted to keep one eye on this remarkable woman, especially around the card table. If she was as intelligent and crafty as she was beautiful, he'd have his work cut out for him.

In his right boot was all the money he possessed in the world. He needed his stake if he was to make enough money to fund his next move, so he had to get it dry before the gathering.

There was a loud rap on the door.

He crossed the room and opened the door to find Mrs. Smart with a pile of working men's clothing...about as far from the fine silks he'd acquired in San Francisco as a man could get. But the clothes were dry and clean, and for that he was grateful.

After he won additional money for his stake at the poker gathering, he'd obtain proper attire. He hoped the gathering would go on as scheduled, which might be hard given the devastating fire

"These should hold you, Mr. Scott. At least for now. And there's a towel at the bottom of the pile. When Miss Kelly announces your turn in the bath, I'll make sure the water's changed before you bathe." She handed the clothing to him.

A dimple appeared in Tyler's right cheek as he smiled, and his dark eyes sparkled. "Thank you, Mrs. Smart. I very much appreciate your assistance in these troubled times."

She chuckled brightly. "Don't expect me to fall under the spell of your considerable charms, Mr. Scott. Mr. Smart and I have been happily married many a year—I've met many a handsome card player such as yourself and survived each encounter."

Tyler smiled as Mrs. Smart closed the door to his room, leaving him alone. He moved to the window overlooking the street and saw the residents purposefully moving through the desolate, smoking ruins of the once-proud frontier town. Makeshift shelters framed with lumber, the roof and walls made of blankets and canvas scrounged from the few remaining buildings, were being erected over the charred rubble. People were picking their way through the embers attempting to salvage whatever they could. He saw some children playing and chasing each other between the stands of blackened wood. This was a hardy community that would soon rise from the ashes like the phoenix.

His thoughts were interrupted by a knock on his door and a muffled voice. *It was Victoria Kelly*. The sound of her voice rose as if carried by a gentle breeze.

"Mr. Scott, I've finished my bath. Mrs. Smart says yours will be ready in twenty minutes."

Tyler moved to the door and pressed one hand flat against it. "Thank you, Miss Kelly." he said, then listened intently to hear her speak again. For a second he thought he could hear her gentle breathing. This was followed by the sound of her slippered footsteps retreating and the opening and closing of her door.

"We shall see each other again, Miss Kelly," he murmured, "very soon."

***

After his shave and bath, Tyler returned to his room and put on the clothing Mrs. Smart had given him. Gray woolen pants, a white rough cotton shirt, and black boots.

He left the room and went to the lobby where he found Hank Smart using a corn broom to sweep out an accumulation of gray ash that had been tracked in from the fire. The main doors were open to the fresh breeze blowing in from the bay, sending the smoke into the valley away from the city. It allowed Hank a chance to air out the hotel and to sweep the dust onto the street. He paused and leaned on his broom when he noticed Tyler on the stairs.

Tyler smiled thinly and nodded. He hadn't worn such attire since he was a boy living in the working-class neighborhood of Boston where he grew up.

"Well, Mr. Scott, don't we look like the citified one," Hank said with a twinkle in his eye.

Tyler nodded politely. "Thank you for these." He ran his hands down the sides of the pants.

"When is the gathering to start?" Tyler needed to pay these good people for their hospitality, and his precious stake could be easily consumed in short order if he stayed too long and used it for room and board. He expected the current local situation would make for some interesting creative capitalism.

Hanks eyebrows arched. "A little anxious, are we?" He chuckled, not expecting an answer, then dropped his gaze to the floor. Hank began to sweep again, creating a new dust cloud of soft, gray flakes that followed him wherever he stepped.

Tyler buried his hands in the pockets of his trousers and leaned against the smooth, dark wood of the staircase railing. He felt he should offer to help. Opening his mouth to speak, he heard a woman's voice call his name from somewhere above him. He turned and looked up the carpeted stairs to see the most beautiful woman he had ever seen descending toward him. His heart pounded hard in his chest as his mouth became dry.

"Mr. Scott." Victoria gave him a slight nod as she swept down the stairs. Her wide blue eyes sparkled and she smelled of fresh lavender. She looked lovely. Her blonde hair was worn up, and her simple blouse and skirt, which drifted about her, made it look as if she floated on a cloud. She smiled warmly as she slid past him then turned her attention to Mr. Smart.

"Is there a place to have a meal in your establishment, Mr. Smart?" Victoria asked. Hank grinned easily at her, then looked at Tyler. "Certainly, Miss Kelly. We have a small dining area off the lobby to the left of the front desk. If you have a seat I'll call my wife."

"Thank you, sir." She nodded her head slightly to acknowledge Mr. Smart's instructions then, with a swish of her skirts, walked toward the front desk.

She suddenly stopped and turned to face Tyler. "Would you care to join me, Mr. Scott? I hate to eat alone."

He was startled to hear her offer. "Certainly, Miss Kelly. It would be my honor."

She smiled briefly, turned and walked away, with Tyler following her. The dining room was very small and composed of three tables, each covered with a pale peach tablecloth and surrounded by four plain pine chairs. As Victoria and Tyler entered they were greeted by Emily Smart, who was busy setting two sets of cutlery and two earthenware plates on a table by a window overlooking the street. The polished steel knives, forks, and spoons rested upon neatly-folded white linen napkins.

She looked up they approached. "I heard you speaking with Hank. You set yourselves here and I'll fetch some hot coffee from the kitchen."

Victoria stood in front of her seat and waited for Tyler to hold her chair for her. He nodded, pulled the seat out, made sure she was comfortable, then seated himself. They sat waiting in an uncomfortable silence, looking around the room, until Mrs. Smart returned with a tin coffee pot and two tin cups. "Sorry, but this is all we have ready at the moment. Our good china has yet to be unpacked," she explained.

"That'll be fine." Victoria smiled as Mrs. Smart set the cups on the table.

Mrs. Smart filled the two cups with steaming black coffee, then hurried from the room through the swinging door to the kitchen. Each time the door swung open, there was the unmistakable aroma of frying bacon.

Tyler watched Victoria out of the corner of his eye as she gazed out the window, watching the city residents busying themselves getting their city back in order. Teams of horses drew heavy wagons piled high with charred wood, their owners calling out loudly, urging them on.

Tyler was impressed with the community effort being displayed outside. *The city will take shape again very quickly at this rate.*

He kept his eyes averted from Victoria until he could restrain himself no longer. Stealing a glance at his companion, he caught himself staring at the vibrant beauty sitting across from him. He felt a hard ball in the pit of his belly, and his loins stirred, reactions he hadn't had in a long time. She ignited a fiery passion within him he thought long dead. Ever since he had been rejected by the woman he asked to marry him, he'd felt nothing for women.

"Enjoying the view?" Victoria suddenly asked, turning her eyes toward him. He detected the hint of amusement in her eyes and her tone of voice.

"Sorry, Miss Kelly—I meant no offense." He dropped his gaze to the empty plate.

"So, Mr. Scott, what do you wish to talk about?" She rested her forearms on either side of her plate and intertwined her fingers as she stared at him quizzically.

"Perhaps I should tell you a little about myself," he began.

"No," she said with a suddenness that startled him. "Let me guess."

He nodded slowly as he arched one eyebrow and waiting, looked at her.

"You originate from Boston. You are from a working-class family, and you travel the western-most parts of North America in search of fame and fortune."

Tyler smirked. "Not bad. Though actually I'm a professional gambler. May I ask how you know so much about me? Surely a lady of such obvious refinement wouldn't know much about a peasant like myself."

She smiled briefly. "I've spent a lot of time in Boston. True, most of my time was not spent among the common folk—rather, among the upper classes. But I have been around working class people often enough that I recognize the accent when I hear it."

"If you'll excuse me, miss, I feel I must correct you on one point. America has no class system. There are two types of people in my country--those who have and those who do not."

Victoria laughed merrily, obviously enjoying the conversation. She had opened her full lips to offer a rebuttal when Mrs. Smart returned with the steaming coffee pot and two plates of fried eggs and bacon, which she placed before them. The heady smells coming from the food made Tyler's stomach rumble. The coffee alone had done little to quench his hunger.

"It smells wonderful, Mrs. Smart," said Tyler. "Though I was wondering if you might have a nip of brandy to remove the last of the chill of the ocean water from my bones."

Mrs. Smart smiled tolerantly. "Young man, our bartender, Willie, has just rescued two fine kegs of strong drink from the fire, and is bringing them to the hotel later for the gathering. I don't approve of drink myself, but Hank insists it is the tradition of the game that drink be available for those who desire such things. For now there'll be none available. So you'll have to wait."

She turned and disappeared into the kitchen.

Victoria, her eyes focused on her plate, stopped eating. She wore a deep frown that wrinkled her gentle brow. Tyler looked at her and wondered if he might have somehow offended her.

"Is something wrong, Miss Kelly?" he asked.

"No, nothing," she replied in a soft, clipped tone. She pushed her half-eaten food away then stood, her eyes averted, and hurried from the room. He was so startled he didn't even have time to react, to stand as he should when a lady leaves the room.

Tyler sat for several seconds, blinking, then stood. He pushed aside his bewilderment as Hank rushed into the room, his eyes wild.

"They're gonna hang Abner." Hank gasped for breath as he spoke.

"Who?"

"Abner Rourke, the man who started the fire."

Six

VICTORIA SLAMMED THE door behind her and fell across the bed, her vision clouded by tears. *What kind of fool am I that I should be attracted to a man who drinks?* It was bad enough her father expected her to marry such a man, but to be smitten by such a blackguard, here, in this remote city…*why?*

Her thoughts were interrupted by the sound of angry shouts coming through the partially open window that overlooked the street. She rose into a sitting position as she wiped the tears from her face. Only then did she cross the room to the window. What she saw made her breath catch in her throat.

A mob of angry, shouting people pushed a rotund man, his hands tied behind his back, down the street. He stumbled and nearly fell as two burly men at the head of the mob pushed him until he stood upright. The man cried out for someone named Elizabeth. No one responded.

It was clear that the enraged townspeople were not taking this man out for tea. His balding head was battered and bloodied, and his pale gray work shirt, ripped and streaked with soot and blood, hung half out over his belt.

Victoria suspected what they intended to do with him and wondered how the chief constable would handle the situation.

Even if he did have a police force upon which to draw, she suspected they were ill-equipped to handle this sudden outburst of violence from so many people.

She stepped away from the window and decided to act. Lawless behavior violated her sense of justice, it was something that angered her. This was not right or acceptable in her world.

She opened the door and rushed into the hallway. She paused to consider seeking assistance and went downstairs to find Hank Smart and Tyler coming out of the dinning room.

"Have you seen?" Victoria looked at the two men.

"We heard." Tyler nodded grimly, while Smart's eyes were filled with fear.

"We have to do something." Victoria looked back at the stairs.

"You wait here," Tyler said to her, then turned to look at Smart. "This is no matter for a woman."

Victoria felt the heat rise in her cheeks. *How dare he!*

"I can handle myself in any situation, sir." Her eyes burned with the fire of her convictions. She locked eyes with Tyler. "I'm a champion horsewoman and can out run and out swim you. I can also handle a rifle better then most men, so don't just dismiss me."

Tyler's frown and pressed lips said he was skeptical of her abilities and claims, although he knew that some of it was true.

She ignored the two men and headed for the front door. The three of them got to the lobby in time to see the mob arrive at a tall, lonely oak tree still standing outside the front of the hotel.

The chief constable, with two volunteers next to him, stood at the base of the tree, attempting to stop the lynching.

Victoria, Tyler, and Smart headed into the street and walked toward the tree.

"Who is he?" Victoria whispered as she asked Mr. Smart.

"His name is Abner Rourke. He owns the feed store. Rumor has it he started the fire."

"Did he?"

Hank gaped at her as if to ask what difference it made. "I don't know," he said, caution evident in his voice.

"Let's assume he did."

Hank glanced at Tyler, who shrugged.

The leader of the lynching party was exchanging angry words with the chief constable. Chief Constable McNalley was using every inch of his six-foot-plus frame and broad shoulders to deter the man, even though he was severely outnumbered by the angry mob.

"There'll be no hangin' today." McNalley looked directly into the face of a man carrying a coil of rope over one shoulder. Behind him stood a motley collection of thirty men, all shouting Abner's name and demanding the chief constable stand aside. Their shouts were clear to Victoria.

"He burned my house."

"My children nearly died."

"I lost a dog."

"Let's hang him."

This is going to be a tough situation. The chief constable desperately needed some backup. Victoria peered up the street. *There has to be someone who can help defuse this situation.*

"Mr. Smart, who are those men down the street with Mayor Diller?" Victoria asked Smart.

"Two of his city counselors—the weasel of a man is named Sims, and the other is Walters."

Sims was a tall, slender-looking man and Walters had a big bushy mustache.

They stood at a safe distance watching the events unfold, doing nothing to stop the lynching.

Victoria was familiar with the names. Diller and his gang of cutthroats were well known to her father. If she played her cards now, she'd blow her cover, even though a man's life hung in the balance. There had to be another way.

Diller had been the foreman who led the work gangs that built the British Columbia leg of the railroad. Some called it the national dream. But many Chinese lives had been sacrificed making the railroad a reality. To Victoria, the thought of all those victims sickened her. They were more than individual lives, they were men with families who loved them. And would probably never know what happened to them.

Victoria wasn't about to let this man be a scapegoat to keep the city's lack of preparedness under wraps. If these folks wanted to vent their anger and frustration, they should direct it at the ones in charge—not at an innocent merchant who simply made a mistake.

A city of almost eleven thousand people with no fire department or equipment to stop such a catastrophe was positively scandalous. The city demanded and received taxes from the shops, bars, and hotels in town, but had yet to deliver on their promises to set up a fire department or a proper police force with a building, manpower, and equipment.

Father suspected Diller and his crowd of thieves were skimming funds wherever they could, which is why he hated the idea of making Vancouver the terminus for his railroad.

"Chief Constable!" Victoria called out as she pushed her way down the dirty street through the throng of men, who surprisingly stood aside to let her pass.

She reached the front of the crowd and turned to face their startled looks. Hank and Tyler slowly moved through the crowd, who stood there as if they were statues in a Greek tragedy, careful not to disturb those they passed until they, too, stood at the front of the crowd.

Victoria frowned when she saw the amused, lopsided grin on Tyler's face. Then both Tyler and Hank turned to face the crowd, standing in front of Victoria, guarding her.

She regarded the assembly of would-be murderers. She spoke in a loud, clear voice. "The chief constable is doing his duty. If this man has done wrong then he will be duly punished within the law."

"The law will not bring back our homes!" shouted a man with red hair the color of carrots and massive arms that were built by hard labor. His shirt sleeves were rolled up to his elbows and she could see the rippling muscles. As he spoke, his face turned the color of pickled beets.

"I've lost everything!" yelled a rotund man at the front of the crowd.

"Where are my children going to sleep? How am I going to feed them?" wailed a woman in the back.

Victoria stood next to Chief Constable McNalley and held up her hands to silence the mob, but they yelled louder and got angrier. As the mob started to press forward, she moved closer to the chief constable. She looked down and saw that he had a pistol in a leather holster on his hip. She reached down, flipped the leather flap to one side, quickly drew it out and fired it over the crowd.

"Enough. All of you clear out and let the police do their jobs!" Victoria's eyes were hard and her mouth a grim line as she looked around, waiting for someone to speak.

Her gaze didn't waver, but held steady. The crowd looked at each other, shook their heads, and shrugged. Their anger was dissipating. They'd lost and they knew it.

"This man will not be lynched." Victoria spoke with firm conviction.

McNalley moved behind Rourke, cut the rope at his wrists, then stood next to Victoria. She smiled at Rourke, held one arm out for him to take as if he were her escort to a grand ball. He appeared doubtful until McNally nodded at him, then linked his arm with Victoria's as they started toward the hotel and, hopefully, safety. Victoria hoped they would make it to the hotel without incident and give the chief constable time to sort the mess out without violence.

Rourke might make it through this day. A lot depended on the mob buying her argument and upon the chief constable's words.

She stopped in her tracks when she heard a piercing nasal voice she recognized. She winced, took a deep breath, then turned to face a man in a black suit holding a leather-bound Bible high over his head.

"That man has sinned!" Parson Sloan's heavy eyebrows knit together above his piercing eyes. With one thin hand, he pointed at Abner as if he were the devil incarnate.

Victoria sighed. *What am I going to do now?*

***

Philip Walker and his wife Connie smelled the smoke while they were still a long way from Vancouver. The smoke seemed to get heaver and denser the closer they got.

Fire in their Hearts

As they came around a curve in the road, set high on a mountain pass, they had a perfect view of the ocean, city, and mountains—and sat in the passenger seat of their open buggy, stunned into silence by the view in front of them.

Their city was a blackened forest of burnt timbers standing against the blue sky. Their home might be gone, too. They urged the driver to hurry the horses. The wagon bumped down the trail next to the bay at breakneck speed.

Connie looked at the city, her Vancouver, and her stomach clenched. Victoria, she had to find Victoria. If something had happened to that girl she'd never forgive herself.

Hiram had asked Philip to watch over his daughter and of course he would, but she loved Victoria, she was like a daughter to her.

Connie chastised herself, she should have stayed to greet Victoria, but they had only gone to New Westminster for a few days. Besides, she didn't really know why Victoria was coming to Vancouver. Connie had invited her to stay with them, of course, but she felt there was another reason Victoria was here.

She did her best to steer clear of the politics surrounding Philip and his job as head of the Canadian Pacific Railroad in Vancouver, especially with all the talk and speculation of where the terminus was going to go, but she was concerned about his job, after all, it would affect their future, too.

She'd hear the talk from the other people, especially the women in town, who wanted the Canadian Pacific Railroad to come to Vancouver. They needed to deter the efforts by Diller and his henchmen to bring the railhead to New Westminster. What they needed to discover was why Sloan was so against Vancouver.

But right now what she needed to do was find Victoria and get her home to safety.

Connie saw Victoria as they arrived in town. She was standing in the street outside one of the few buildings remaining that wasn't a heap of charred wood.

They rushed to Victoria. Connie grabbed her around the shoulders as she hugged her. They were both speaking at once and laughed, the tension easing now that they had found Victoria.

Diller and Smart come to join them.

Connie had heard about Sloan, it was logical to assume that Sloan, a self-appointed religious leader, was behind the impromptu uprising. He'd been trouble since he arrived from the gold fields of the Yukon. Rumor had it he'd attempted to pit two factions against each other and take over the town of Dawson Creek. Fortunately, a group of local prospectors, seeing their profits about to be consumed in a holy war, abducted the parson in the middle of the night and deposited him on the first ship headed south. That ship docked in Vancouver; Sloan disembarked and never left.

Shortly upon his arrival he set up his makeshift church in the back of Rourke's feed store. The towns people immediately suspected that Sloan wanted the store as a base for his operations.

Philip turned and stepped toward the mob with his eyes focused on the religious leader, glaring at him. Philip was rewarded by a look of concern in Sloan's gray eyes.

"I suggest you listen to this young woman and cease this foolish talk of lynching immediately," Philip spoke in a loud clear voice as he spoke to the crowd.

Every face in the crowd betrayed their surprise and confusion.

"Women do not run this city," said Sloan, accompanied by a few bobbing male heads.

Connie watched Victoria as she looked around. It seemed that she was getting more and more nervous. She smoothed her hands on her dress and licked her lips, something Connie knew that Victoria only did when she was nervous.

Philip surveyed the crowd and managed to stare them down. "Everyone listen!. You all know me, I'm the representative for the Canadian Pacific Railroad in Vancouver as well as a member of the City Council. We need law and order. Vancouver is a newly incorporated city and we are proud of her. It's up to the courts to decide on the fate of Mr. Rourke, not us. Now let's go and let the police do their work."

Connie watched the crowd as their anger was defused and they calmed.

"Good, they're listening to Phllip," Victoria said to Connie.

Connie saw that Philip's words had the desired effect when Mayor Diller acted. Until now Diller had stood off at a safe distance, listening intently, waiting for the wind of public opinion to shift. Suddenly, with a burst of speed that surprised her, he rushed to the head of the mob.

"Now, Philip, there's no need to get so worked up. I'm sure that between the chief constable and myself we can bring everything under control."

Sloan dropped his arms to his side and glared at Philip. "If you guarantee God's justice will be served then I bow to your will. I will ask my flock to stand down and let justice take its course."

Philip shuddered.

Connie quickly told Victoria that Sloan was an evil influence on the city, but that Philip had been unable to unmask the parson for the charlatan he was. It seemed Sloan had many strong supporters among the mostly good and honest townsfolk.

McNalley moved forward to take Rourke by one arm and lead him to the makeshift tent used to shelter the police department. His two new deputies had scrounged some wool blankets to construct the temporary structure.

Connie watched McNalley walk away with his prisoner. The fear was evident in Rourke's eyes. She knew that he'd barely escaped hanging today, and he wasn't in the clear yet.

The crowd dispersed slowly, grumbling amongst themselves, clearly disappointed with the decision. Sloan had disappeared as if he were a ghost. The man knew when to play his hand and when to fold and leave, confirming Connie's instincts about him.

Victoria turned to face Philip and Connie Walker, who both looked tired and worn. Their eyes were hooded, their mouths were drawn into thin lines.

Connie stepped forward to embrace Victoria, pleased when her expression eased to one of restrained pleasure. "I'm relieved you're safe, Victoria."

"I agree," Tyler came to stand beside Victoria, his brown eyes watchful.

Victoria broke Connie's embrace and stared at the gambler. "Where were you?" she asked, her tone scornful.

"Why, waiting to see if you needed rescuing. After all, Miss Kelly, you assured me you could handle any situation." Tyler shrugged then looked at Connie with a twinkle in his deep brown eyes.

She frowned. *He's right. I've been the arrogant one, not him.*

Connie looked at the tall, dark man, "Victoria, who is this man?"

"His name is Tyler Scott. He's a vagabond gambler," said Victoria, contempt evident in her voice.

Connie stood tall and faced Tyler, stepping between them to shield Victoria, her expression hard and her eyes cold. "Miss Kelly is a betrothed woman, sir. She has no need of your assistance. We will care for her," she added, remembering her manners.

"Thank you for you concern."

Tyler took a step backward, bowing his head slightly, and tipped his hat. A gentle smile played on his lips. "I'm pleased to be of assistance, ma'am."

Connie slipped one arm around Victoria's waist as they headed for the carriage. They stepped up into the carriage. Victoria casually glanced back in Tyler's direction before the driver urged the horses on. Connie saw that Philip had noticed Victoria's glance as well.

***

Victoria sat ramrod straight in the carriage, close to Connie, keeping her gaze averted from Connie's studied expression. Connie held a regal bearing, as always, having been born into a wealthy and cultured eastern family. Her father, Mr. Randolph Brown of Boston, was old money who had made his fortune in trading with Europe. His fleet of ships provided an important link between the Americas and Europe.

Victoria took Connie's hands in hers. Long ago, at least it seemed to be very long ago, when Victoria lived in her father's home, the Walkers had been good friends to her.

She was very fond of the childless couple—in particular Connie Walker, who had always been a mentor to her.

"Victoria." Connie wrapped the young woman in another warm embrace. Victoria felt the woman's body tremble with emotion as she held her tightly.

"Victoria, I understand that you think you were helping, speaking out in defense of Mr. Rourke, but that is no way for a proper young woman to behave," said Philip, shaking his head, his ruddy features locked in grim determination.

Victoria felt Connie squeeze her hands and gave her a slight nod. She remained quiet.

Victoria remembered that Mr. Philip Walker married Miss Constance Brown at the urging of their wealthy parents to unite two great and powerful families. The Walker fortune was made in the fur trade. It was truly a corporate merger.

This had occurred long before Victoria was born, however. By the time Victoria met the Walkers and came to know them, the Walker's marriage was far more than a unification of wealth and power, it was a unification of two hearts. Connie and Philip were truly in love and had been since they first met all those years ago.

They were now her dearest friends. Victoria thought of Connie, if not as a surrogate mother, then, at the very least, as an older sister.

Victoria glanced into Connie's calm, concerned, sea green eyes that watched her in silence.

"I'm fine, Connie." Victoria made an effort to look around her as they traveled.

"That's not what we need to discuss and you know it."

"What then?"

"Enough of this. This is not the time nor the place," interrupted Philip sternly, with a meaningful glance toward the driver.

The two women fell silent. Instead they watched the people they passed who were busy scrounging through the burned-out buildings and rigging makeshift lean-tos to house themselves until proper buildings could be built.

Victoria sat even straighter on the hard carriage seat, pulling her shoulders back as she looked at the mountains they were driving through.

She realized she could hear bird song again and the smell of smoke was now almost non-existent. Instead the air was heavy with the fresh scent of the pine and cedar trees all around them. She could taste them. She took a deep breath through her mouth, held it, than slowly let it out through her nose. This was the best exercise to clear out the last of the smoke in her lungs.

Philip smiled at Connie and Victoria when a three-story house appeared on the horizon. Freshly painted an ivory white with blue gray trim, it was a beacon of civilization in an otherwise rough-hewn world. There was no finer home in the city.

They stopped before the large front porch surrounding the lower level. There were three steps that led to the double glass and wood doors of the main entrance. Twin solid brass door handles gleamed in the afternoon sun.

The second floor extended to cover the lower level, held aloft by large timbers than ran down the side of the porch then buried deep into the ground, giving the structure its solid framing.

The driver leapt to the ground and held the horses steady as the trio disembarked. Philip turned to the driver. "Thank you."

The driver nodded and led the horses away, the hoofs clopping their usual steady beat, stomping the brown earth as they disappeared around the side of the house.

Connie drew one arm around the younger woman's shoulder then led her up the stairs to the door. Victoria let herself be warmed by the embrace and relaxed.

A woman with dark skin the color of coffee with heavy cream, wearing a maid's uniform, met Victoria, Connie, and Philip at the front door. She held the door open for them, her warm, dark eyes gazing at the two women and her white teeth gleaming as she smiled at them. Philip followed his wife and Victoria into the house.

As the maid closed the door behind them the glass insert in the front door rattled softly in the silent room.

It was later in the day and the setting sun was streaming into the foyer of the home. Rich scents of wood polish and beeswax candles filled the air.

An oak Grandfather clock, enclosed in a glass and brass case, ticked loudly. The deep burgundy silk carpet beneath their feet absorbed the sound of their footsteps.

"Anna," sighed Connie, "it's so good to see a kind face. Victoria, this is Anna, our maid, and Anna, this is Miss Victoria."

"There is some mail for you, Mr. & Mrs. Walker, and there might be some for you, too, miss," the maid told them as she bowed her head and curtseyed as if she had been trained in the finest of European homes. Victoria nodded to the maid and felt a warmth coming from her that made her feel safe.

Through the windows Victoria saw that the afternoon shadows had already lengthened. She shifted her gaze to the large ticking clock. It was after six o'clock in the afternoon already. Where has the day gone?

Weariness overcame Victoria, her knees felt suddenly weak. She felt her empty stomach rumble in protest. "Haven't we missed tea?" she asked Connie, trying to cover up the slight noise. Victoria had had a light lunch after her bath, but no breakfast due to all the excitement and she was getting very hungry.

"I think the Empire will survive." Connie grinned at her.

Now it was Victoria's turn to offer a weak grin. Her eyes closed. "The Empire might survive, but I think I need a rest and a bite to eat, although I'm not sure which I need more or first. Also, I'd like to see my mail, I'm sure there're letters from Herbert and Father for me."

Connie's expression changed to one of concern. She glanced at her husband who was hanging his outer coat in the hall closet. He looked back at her with a dark frown clouding his features, his gray eyes hard as forged steel.

"I'll get the post for you, Victoria, and then we'll let you rest," Connie said as she went to retrieve Victoria's mail.

"Connie, we have much to discuss," Philip said as he reached into the inside pocket of his jacket to extract a white envelope with a broken red wax seal. Upon seeing the envelope, Connie's face paled.

Connie went to the hall table and brought back two envelopes, one white and one tan, and gave them to Victoria.

Victoria saw the white one was from her father and had his red wax seal on them. It was the same as the one Philip had shown Connie. She also suspected that the tan one was from the government and had information she had requested. She was tired, but at the sight of the envelopes she could hardly wait to open them.

Connie nodded to her husband then led the weary young woman to the gleaming wooden staircase that led to the rooms on the upper floors.

***

Victoria sat down in front of the dressing table and pulled out the letters she had received, then Connie appeared at her door. "Here you go, honey. I've gathered a few things for you to wear until we get a chance to go into New Westminster and do some shopping. The dress will have to be altered a little, but we can take care of that. Are you going to lie down for a bit?"

"Yes. Oh, and you've packed a couple of nightgowns, they look beautiful," Victoria said as she smiled at her friend and felt the soft texture of the material.

Connie gave Victoria a quick hug and left the room. Victoria closed the door and went back to her letters.

She opened the tan one first, it was from the City of Vancouver and contained a list of the major real estate owners of Vancouver. She quickly scanned the list and was surprised to see that of the top twenty-five names listed, the Canadian Pacific Railroad was first with one million acres listed. A couple of others caught her attention, too, Dr. Milne with fifteen thousand acres, C. Walker with ten thousand, and Mr. Sloan with five thousand acres.

Next to Mr. Sloan's listing was a note indicating that his property had been transferred to the Crown in exchange for ten thousand acres in New Westminster.

Interesting, very interesting. Why and how did the Canadian Pacific Railroad get that much land, unless they were going to make Vancouver the terminus city? She was also surprised at the amounts indicated for individuals. C. Walker, was that Connie Walker? And Mr. Sloan, could that be the good Reverend Sloan?

The other letter was from her father, telling her news from home and that he missed her. She would have a lot to tell him when she saw him next.

Seven

TYLER ENTERED THE bright comfortable lobby of the Brighton Hotel followed closely by Hank Smart. They were met by an anxious Emily Smart, who wrapped her arms around her husband as soon as he was inside. She broke their embrace, quickly pressing her lips to his. "Hank, I'm so glad you're all right."

Hank held his wife close and murmured something about everything being okay and this being completely inappropriate as he let her go.

Tyler stood watching the reunion of husband and wife with a bland expression. Emily frowned at him. "Don't you believe in love, Mr. Scott?" she said.

He shrugged. "As much as I believe I can make an inside straight."

Emily shook her head, looked up at Hank, then pressed her face into her husband's right shoulder.

Tyler sighed and felt an odd twinge of regret for having been so flippant. His recent feelings for Victoria had really confused him. But it wasn't only passion he felt for her. He'd felt passion for women before, it was something else. Somehow he felt they were bound together, soul mates.

He knew in his heart his feelings for her ran deeper than he would have liked, though he was loath to admit it, even to himself.

"Is the saloon open, Mr. Smart?" Tyler said in a loud voice, interrupting the scene that made him feel envious of the bond between the couple.

"The bar's open, Mr. Scott," said Hank, his eyes locked on his wife's. One arm was around her waist while the other directed the gambler toward the dining area. "Once you go through the dining room there's a door that connects to the barroom at the rear of the hotel. My bartender, Willie, should be in there serving by now. I expect there's more than a few dry throats being quenched."

Tyler nodded, although at the moment neither Hank nor Emily were paying any attention to him. He headed through the dining room into the bar through a plain wooden door with a brass handle. As he walked inside he found the room dimly lit and it took several seconds for his eyes to adjust.

Finally he was able to see the surroundings clearly. It was like any of the establishments he'd left behind on the Barbary Coast in San Franciso.

Behind the bar was a dusky-skinned man with a clean, hairless scalp who stood with a lopsided grin pasted on his dark features. He was diligently wiping a glass with a plain, clean, white towel. He wore the dress common to most bartenders Tyler had encountered: a plain white shirt, black pants, vest, and black bow tie, with a plain white apron completing his ensemble.

There were a number of round wooden tables surrounded by curved high back chairs. A few of the tables contained some of the thirsty locals with either a foam-topped beer or a glass of whiskey in front of them as they played cards. For the first time since arriving in Vancouver, Tyler felt at home.

He grinned at the bartender as he ambled up to the bar. Taking a place along the bar he rested one booted foot on the brass rail that guarded the bar's base.

"Howdy, what can I get ya?" The bartender's dark eyes traveled over Tyler as if sizing him up, the grin still on his face.

Tyler leaned forward on the bar, his elbows resting on the polished wood surface, his fingers locked together. "You're not from around these parts. Where are you from?" Tyler casually looked at the mirror behind the bar.

The bartender's eyes shifted to Tyler's, a look of suspicion crossing his face, and his eyes narrowed slightly. The grin turned down at the corners of his wide mouth as he stopped cleaning the glass he was holding. "New York. Sir."

Tyler broke into a wide smile. "Always nice to run into a fellow American. I'm from Boston, myself." Tyler stuck out his hand across the bar in greeting.

The bartender, seeing the offered hand, relaxed his shoulders and gripped Tyler's hand firmly. Tyler shook the man's hand with such enthusiasm that the bartender's grin faded to a wary expression.

Tyler chuckled lightly. "Don't worry, friend—a long tradition of abolitionist blood courses through my veins. I believe Mr. Smart called you Willie. My name's Tyler, Tyler Scott."

A slow smile spread over Willie's features. "Pleased to meet you, Mr. Scott." They each let go of the other's hand simultaneously.

"So what's your poison?"

Tyler chuckled. "Somehow I doubt that I'll find it in this kinda place." He raised one eyebrow at Willie, who grinned even more widely.

"We have some very good Scottish whiskey which I'm certain you will find to your liking."

"What, no bourbon?"

It was Willie's turn to chuckle. "I do keep a couple of bottles of the sour mash in the back, just in case someone of our nationality and inclination comes by. Don't get much call for the stuff here in the land of Empire Loyalists."

Some of the men seated at the table nearest the bar looked up from their cards to glare at the two men. Tyler caught the look and nodded to the four men closest to them, who grumbled and went back to their game.

"What's their problem?" he asked Willie in a hushed tone.

"Don't mind them, sir. They're still some hard feelings about the Yukon thing, ya know?"

Tyler shook his head. "Sorry, no, I don't know anything about the gold rush. I just look for men fresh from the gold fields to see if they're interested in playing a friendly game of cards."

A burly man seated at the table stood abruptly. His fists were clenched and his face red with rage. "That'll be enough, Yank," he growled, his waxed, handlebar mustache trembled with his words.

Tyler turned around and faced the angry man. He leaned back, his elbows resting behind him on the bar, a lopsided grin on his face. If the angry man had paused to take note, Tyler's shoulders were loose, his legs planted wide to maintain balance, and his blue eyes calm, filled with determination. A sure sign he'd easily be able to deflect any attacker. He was also quite adept at inflicting painful injury if necessary.

The man was a head taller than Tyler and heavily muscled. His arms rippled, his massive chest heaved as he took a deep breath and moved toward Tyler. His eyes bore into Tyler's. If it were possible his angry glare would've cut Tyler down where he stood.

Fire in their Hearts

The man neared Tyler and as his foul booze breath wafted over him, Tyler gagged.

As the man got close, Tyler planted his left leg and brought his right knee up into the man's groin, while using his arms to pull the man by his shoulders toward him, taking him off-balance. Air burst from his lungs and his eyes went wide. He yelped in pain as he fell heavily to the wooden floor with a loud thump. There was silence in the room.

His fellow players, who'd been watching the drama unfolding from the comfort of their seats, looked shocked and horrified. Their earlier expressions had said they fully expected their friend to pound the stranger into the floor like a dull nail into a board. They stared at each other, clearly dumfounded by the outcome.

Now they pushed back their chairs, scraping loudly on the floor. As they stood, there was an audible click of a shotgun hammer being brought into place. Tyler glanced behind the bar and saw Willie with a double-barreled shotgun pointing toward the three men. Both barrels were locked and ready.

"The nigger's only got two barrels," growled one of the men.

"So, which two of you want to die?" asked Willie. He swept the long, blue steel twin barrels back and forth over the men.

One of the men looked sheepish and sat down. "Com'on, boys, let's get back to our game. The Yank ain't worth it."

As the men sat down, Willie lowered the shotgun, turned and replaced it in the rack beneath the bar. "Insurance." He turned back to Tyler and smiled.

Tyler grinned, too, nodded, then bent over the man who lay moaning on the floor grasping his bruised manhood. "You okay?"

"Yes, sir," the man replied between gritted teeth.

"Good, then get up and go back to your game." Tyler held out one hand and helped the injured man to his feet.

The man limped to his seat and sat, his features twisted as he winced from the pain.

"You in, Bill?" asked one of the men, his eyes drifting over his injured companion then back to the table.

The red-faced man grunted. While one hand cradled his damaged privates, he used the other to toss in a coin from the short pile in front of him.

Tyler turned to face Willie. "Do you often get excitement in here?"

Willie shrugged, placed a shot glass on the bar, and filled it with amber liquid in one smooth motion. A bottle appeared, then disappeared so fast that all Tyler saw was a blur of burnt orange in the dim light that came from between the floor length curtains that covered the windows. *Good thing I don't have to face Will at the card table, he's fast.*

"Mind if I join you, boys," Tyler said cheerfully as he turned back to the card players. He felt like a warm up game before the big game .

The man who'd encouraged Bill to rejoin the game nodded, his face taut. Tyler smiled thinly then moved another chair from an adjoining table to a spot between Bill and one of the other men. They all shifted their chairs over to let him have access to the table. The four men's eyes said they were none too happy to have his company, but they would tolerate him as long as he had money to lose.

"Coffee, Willie, black and strong, just like you." Tyler said with a twinkle in his eye.

Willie grinned at the small joke and left to fetch a mug from the kitchen.

Tyler gazed around the table at the unhappy faces and pressed one index finger against the side of his head.

"Gotta keep the mind clear if you're gonna play cards, don't ya think?" The men nodded somberly.

"Let's play some cards." Tyler reached into his left boot and pulled out a wad of bills, which he slapped on the table. He then reached into his right boot, pulled out a thin dagger, and slapped it on top of the bills. He winked at their stunned expressions. "I love insurance, don't you?"

***

Victoria woke from her deep sleep with a start. Then she remembered she was in Connie's home and relaxed.

The room was cloaked in darkness except for the open window where moonlight shone through, making the golden window frame glow. The linen curtains moved as a gentle evening breeze swirled through the window.

The room smelled of rose water, and she felt at ease for the first time since she began her journey across the empty vastness of Canada.

Prior to leaving Toronto, she'd seen a map of the country, but never imagined the sheer size of the vast, untamed land between the civilized cities. Not that this place could be considered civilized—it was a far cry from what she was accustomed to.

She sat up, blinked to clear the sleep from her eyes. Everything was quiet, no sound reached her ears. She wondered what time it was. It was dark and the moon was out. At this time of year, that meant it was very late.

She swung her legs over the side of the bed, dropping her bare feet to the floor. The hardwood planks creaked as she stood beside the bed.

She was dressed in a nightdress that Connie had loaned her.

She moved to the closet for a dressing gown out of habit, shaking her head as she looked at the simple clothes Mrs. Smart had loaned her. She only had one change of clothing, she really needed to buy some clothes soon.

She dressed and noticed that Connie had been kind enough to include a powder blue knit sweater, which she also pulled on, hooking the row of three buttonhooks to close the front of the sweater.

Luckily she and Connie wore the same shoe size and Connie had given her a pair of boots. Victoria was pleased at how comfortable the old leather was and how well they fit her.

She opened her bedroom door in silence. None of the oil lamps that lined the hallway were lit. There was enough light from the moon coming through the glass doors in the foyer at the bottom of the staircase and she was able to make her way safely down the staircase to the bottom landing.

As she reached for the brass door handle, a soft voice behind her said, "Goin' out, miss? Kinda dark this time a night for a stroll, don't ya think?"

Victoria started and her heart skipped a beat. She turned to see the maid, in a pale pink nightdress with a blue and red plaid wrap around her shoulders, a plain white night cap on her head, standing, watching her. Her long slender arms hung loosely at her waist. Her eyes were wide and curious.

"Anna. I'm going for a walk to get a little fresh air, that's all."

Anna smiled, nodded, then turned to disappear down the hallway left of the stairs.

Fire in their Hearts

Victoria felt her heart slow. Anna had really startled her far more than she was willing to admit. *Odd. Why was she up?*

Victoria opened the door, to be greeted by a warm breeze coming from a westerly direction. She stood in the doorway, closed her eyes, took a deep breath, and drank in the complex smells of the wildflowers that sprang from the edge of the forest to mingle with the scent of the ocean. The rich scents were unlike anything she had ever experienced.

Maybe this would finally clear her nose and mouth of the foul wood smoke that seemed to follow her. She knew she'd barely escaped death only the day before.

While the thought of death didn't bother her—it came to everyone eventually—she knew much of her life was ahead of her. She was convinced that her life's work was yet to come, whatever that might be. She felt that someone or something was just on the edge of her senses, waiting for her.

The journey here, her near-death experience, had made her realize that her destiny did not lie with Herbert Littlefield, but how would she know her destiny when she met him or it?

And what about Tyler Scott, the handsome gambler? He was a man of some experience, but his enjoyment of his vices—drinking and gambling—made him unsuitable not only to her, but most assuredly to her father.

She sighed and stepped outside, closing the door to stand on the porch alone. She heard the sound of the crickets in the grass, the rustle of the leaves in the trees as the wind brushed against them, and in the distance, the soft call of an owl.

She turned to gaze at the white globe that was the moon as it hung in the starry sky. It was brilliant. A welcome beacon in this desolate place.

The moon's smiling face stared down at her as if she was the only person in the world. She'd never felt so alone.

Victoria stepped onto the dusty, dirt road that wound its way into town and started to walk. Except for the odd, jagged pebble, the rich, brown earth, cut by wagon tracks to create two ruts through the forest, was mostly smooth. The breeze tossed her hair as it fanned her face. It was cool and felt good.

With her head bowed in concentration, she hugged her sweater tighter about her slender body, not to protect herself from cold, for it wasn't cold, but to hide from her feelings and her conflicting emotions.

"What's a perty thin' like you doing out here all alone?" A man's deep voice shattered the quiet and interrupted her thoughts. She stopped abruptly and looked up.

In front of her she saw the image of a large-shouldered man silhouetted by the glow of the moon. He wore a wide-brimmed Stetson and a long raincoat. As he stepped forward she could see his lean, haggard features, covered in dark stubble. A long, jagged scar ran down his right cheek. His dark eyes calmly studied her. One rough hand rested on the butt of a pistol in a leather holster that hung off his right hip. At first his words didn't register, then he said, "I said, what's a pretty young thin' like you do'in' out here alone?"

She shook her head. Who was this person? "What business is it of yours?"

The man's smile was hard, and wicked, his eyes deep and narrowed at the corners. *The arrogance.*

He dropped his shoulders, his right hand still resting on his holstered pistol. "You must be Victoria Ann McNichol."

The use of her full, proper name made her start. She struggled to maintain the outward appearance of calm.

Fire in their Hearts

From the corners of her eyes she surveyed the surrounding forest for any possible escape route.

The dark woods on either side of the road might provide a place to get away if she needed to.

"My name is Kelly, Victoria Kelly."

"Sorry, Miss McNichol, we know who you really are."

"So you know my name, what of it?" Her words challenged him.

He gave her a crooked smile then nodded to someone behind her. "Me and the boys think a gal like you will come in handy."

Before she could react she felt a sharp blow to the back of her head, and the moonlight, the smells, and the sounds of the forest disappeared into blackness.

Eight

TYLER LEANED BACK in the wooden chair causing it to creak. The salon was elegant—with polished wooden walls and floor, and an gleaming rosewood piano by the bar that took up the whole of one wall. A couple of other round tables in the salon also had people playing games. Most of the players had a coffee in front of them, and the air was thick and hazy with the smell of smoke. The windows and doors were open to get the fresh air in and the stale air out.

It was getting to be later in the morning and the egg and ham breakfast he'd had was wearing off.

He studied the faces of the three men who sat around his table, all intent on their cards. The dealer, a butcher named Hugh, had just raised the pot by a dollar. Tyler looked down at his cards, he felt some doubt about his hand being the winner this time. In the past hour Hugh hadn't raised a single bet, so why now? *A bluff? A lucky hand?*

He had no tells. The butcher was either surprisingly good at hiding his emotions and his habits, or he had no idea what he was doing.

Tyler placed his cards face down in front of him. He knew what the odds were. He had three threes. Pretty good in stud poker, but these guys allowed only one draw, which changed the odds.

His neighbors, Bill and Carl, had nothing as usual—even if they did, the look in their eyes said they would fold if he pushed back with a solid bet. But Hugh, he was the enigma. *What would he do?*

Tyler decided to push back hard. "Five." The chair dropped onto all four legs as he leaned forward pushing a five dollar bill toward the pot. He leaned back again with his fingers interlocked in his lap. Bill and Carl exchanged glances then tossed their cards into the center. *Two down, one to go.*

Hugh smiled grimly at Tyler, his eyes dancing over at the gambler across from him. Tyler was two hundred dollars up and everyone at the table knew who was the better man.

Tyler smiled broadly at him.

"I don't think you have it," said Hugh.

"You gotta pay to see 'em," Tyler said, his voice calm, even.

Hugh glanced down at the short stack of bills sitting in front of him then he stole a glance at Tyler's much larger stack of bills.

He laid his cards face down and picked up a five dollar bill off his short stack and tossed it on the pile of bills in the middle of the table. "Call."

Tyler smiled and with one hand he flipped his cards over. He looked expectantly at Hugh, who gazed at the three threes. Tyler wasn't surprised to see the color drain from the butcher's face. He'd won the hand. *Sometimes, I even amaze myself.*

Just as Hugh threw his cards down, the door at the other end of the room burst inward to bang hard against the wall. Hank Smart and Mayor Diller came charging into the room as if they were being chased by a mad bull. Hank's scowl made Tyler cringe inside. Something serious was going on.

Hugh flipped his cards onto the table, Tyler couldn't help but smile at the pair of aces and pair of kings. Hank and the mayor marched over to Tyler and stood next to him.

Tyler looked into a Hank's cold serious eyes. What he saw made him close his eyes. "What's wrong?"

"It's Victoria. She's missing and we can't find the constable."

Tyler gazed at the two men with a blank expression. Then a slow frown crossed his face as he nodded, his skin visibly darkening. "When?"

"We don't know. Mr. and Mrs. Walker woke up this morning to find her gone."

Tyler pushed back his chair. He looked at the bartender. "Willie, will you hold my winnings?"

"No problem, Mr. Scott." Willie moved close to the table, leaned over to scoop the money into his apron. "I've gotta safe behind the bar for just such occasions."

Tyler placed one hand Wiilie's shoulder, which caused him to pause to look into the gambler's eyes. Tyler nodded his thanks, then turned to follow Hank and Mayor Diller out the door.

It was about noon, the day warm, the sky bright blue. Tyler rubbed his rough chin. *I need a shave.* "We'll need to speak with the Walkers. Where's the chief constable?"

Diller nodded, looking relieved. "He's at the police tent. Said he's been busy these last few days. He and his constable are guarding the prisoner from the mob. They don't have a jail set up yet, but some of the men are busy building one on Main Street. Once they have the jail done, the chief says he'll start looking for Miss Kelly."

Tyler cast a glance at Hank, who shrugged.

The look in his eye said he wasn't too pleased with the chief constable's attitude or priorities. Neither was Tyler.

"It's okay, Mr. Mayor. Hank and I'll check this out," said Tyler. The mayor nodded, turned, and soon his portly body was headed down the boardwalk away from the two men.

"Let's go."

"Where to?" asked Hank.

Tyler shrugged. "To see the Walkers, of course."

Hank looked doubtful. "Don't you think you should clean up first?"

Tyler rubbed the stubble on his chin again with his long fingers and nodded. "Yup," he said with a sardonic grin. "Now tell me where the Walkers live."

***

Hank drove them out to the Walkers house on the edge of the city in the hotel's supply wagon. On the way there, he told Tyler the Walkers had been away for a few months. He also explained that Philip Walker was the local representative for Hiram McNichol, the most powerful man behind the Canadian National Railroad.

When Tyler saw the house he was impressed such a magnificent house existed in this otherwise rustic setting. It reminded him of some of the finer homes he'd seen in San Francisco, and must be owned by someone with money. He wondered how Victoria Kelly, card player, might know such well-heeled types. This bore a closer examination at their next encounter. He'd have to watch her a little more closely than he had, something didn't quite add up. He had to win at the gathering, and she might stand in his way.

They pulled up in front of the wooden porch, Mr. Philip Walker glowering at them from the porch, waiting as Hank Smart urged the horses to halt, working the reins with evident skill.

Tyler jumped down to land hard on his feet next to the wagon, causing the horses to shift and pull on their collars.

Hank yanked on the reins to steady them.

"Mr. Walker?" asked Tyler as he started up the three wooden steps that led to the porch. He still wore the rustic clothing that Hank and Emily had loaned him, so he was certain he looked more like a drifter than the successful gambler he was.

Philip Walker eyed him with obvious distain, his right hand buried in the pockets of his gray, well-pressed trousers while holding the matching suit jacket in his other hand. Tyler noticed the gleam of a gold watch chain running from a brass button on his vest to a pocket where the top of a watch could be seen. Philip smoothly slid his jacket over his arms and settled it onto his shoulders, then tugged it into place.

"Mr. Scott, why are you here?" asked Philip Walker as Tyler came to the top of the stairs.

"I'm the man who's going to find Miss Kelly for you," Tyler spoke, his voice low and serious, his eyes hard as they fixed on Philip Walker.

"Oh, yes, the gambler."

Philip frowned as he glanced over at Hank, who still sat in the driver's seat of the wagon, his eyes fixed on Philip, watching him intently. Hank's face was grim as he nodded to Philip.

Philip, having made his decision, nodded. "Come in."

He turned and led the way inside as Hank braked the wagon, dropped to the ground, and tied the horses to a hitching post before following Tyler and Philip though the front doors. Once inside, Philip led them into his library off the main foyer. Rows of books in tall oak bookcases lined the walls.

Fire in their Hearts

In the center of the room was an oversized oak desk with a large, ornate glass and brass oil lamp sitting to one side.

Three brown leather, wing-backed chairs were clustered in front of the desk and one rounded, medium back, oak chair sat behind it. Philip sat behind the desk as Hank and Tyler each took a seat across from him.

Sunlight streamed in through two tall, wide windows overlooking the forest of mixed evergreens and deciduous trees. As Tyler looked out the window, he saw a flock of red-breasted robins take flight into the tree branches.

The library was a good-sized room, the main feature a fieldstone fireplace on the exterior wall with an oak mantel. A dark pile of wood ash sat in the fireplace and the hearth had a wood bin with brass appliances next to it. The room smelled vaguely of wood smoke mingled with leather from the books.

Unhurried, Philip eased back in his chair and eyed the two men. He smiled thinly as he reached for a carved wooden box near the front of the desk. He slid open the box and pulled out a fine cigar, turned it around, and offered the cigar box to the two men. Hank smiled as he took one, while Tyler declined with the wave of a hand. Philip calmly studied the men as he bit off the end of his cigar then lit it with a long match he pulled from a desk drawer. The smell and taste of sulfur filled the room, soon followed by the scent of cigar tobacco.

Hank nodded as he accepted the still burning match to light his own cigar. The two men puffed ardently until a cloud of pungent gray smoke filled the air. The odor wasn't unpleasant, but Tyler had never been one for smoking.

He watched Philip as he put the matches back in the drawer and discerned that the man was sizing them up as he would a prize steer.

"Mrs. Walker hates these things. But I enjoy them when I have the company to enjoy them with."

Philip looked at the other two men and waited.

From the way Hank had spoken about Walker, Tyler suspected he was a man to be reckoned with. So far Walker was living up to his billing. He was a hard man to read, even for Tyler, who was an expert at reading people.

Finally Philip removed his cigar from between his lips and placed it in a heavy brass ashtray on his desk. He leaned forward on his elbows to glare at Tyler. "So, Mr. Scott, is it?" Tyler nodded with an easy smile on his lips. "Would you have an idea where Miss Kelly might be?"

It suddenly struck Tyler that Hank had led him out here under false pretenses. He, Tyler, wasn't here to lead or aid in the search for Victoria, he was here as the supposed kidnapper, he was here as a suspect.

Tyler struggled to keep his voice steady as the anger boiled from deep inside. The confidence of Walker's tone and his relaxed manner made it clear they weren't going to look for Victoria, they felt they had the person responsible for her kidnapping right in front of them. Or, at the worst, they had a perfect scapegoat, they could pin the crime on him if she was killed.

His cool eyes focused on Walker's as he tried to stare the wealthy man down. Philip's arrogant tone signaled to Tyler that he'd already been judged and found guilty.

Slowly Tyler folded his hands in his lap and locked his fingers together in order to keep his emotions in check—making sure that he didn't just stand up, deck Walker, and stuff that smile down his throat. He had just finished risking his life to save Victoria's. How did they come to this conclusion? Or was there more to this story that he didn't know about?

If Mr. Walker thought for one second he could so easily intimidate him, a professional gambler, he was about to be proven wrong.

"And why would you think I know anything about the whereabouts of Miss Kelly? If, indeed, that is her real name." His eyes narrowed as he caught a brief glint of doubt in Walker's eyes, then it quickly disappeared.

Philip Walker ignored Tyler. He snatched his cigar from the ashtray, where it left a small gray mound of ash behind. He placed the now unlit cigar between his lips, slid the drawer open to retrieve another match.

Between clenched teeth he said, "We know you spent time with Miss Kelly after the unfortunate fire." Walker lit his cigar and immediately began to puff copious clouds of white smoke into the air. The tip of the cigar flared red. The odor was pleasant, but almost overwhelming in the confined space of the library.

Tyler noted the second attack on his senses in as many minutes. The guy was good, but not good enough to go professional at the tables.

"We formally met at Mr. Smart's hotel after the fire, but Miss Kelly was gracious enough not to let our delayed introductions stop her from saving my life earlier in the day. I owe her a favor or two." Tyler paused to cast a sharp glance at Hank, who averted his gaze to look out the window.

"I'm here to help her if I can. Perhaps you should tell me what you think happened to her, so I can begin my search. I believe time is wasting, don't you?"

Walker looked out the window, took a puff on the cigar, then turned to face him again, placing the cigar in the ashtray. His expression softened and he nodded at Tyler.

He was obviously satisfied with what he'd heard. He nodded once to Hank, dismissing him. Hank stood and left the room, closing the door behind him with a soft click.

"Mr. Scott, what I'm about to tell you must not leave this room, but I think you'll need this information in your search for Victoria. The police are not to be notified or become involved in this matter. Do you understand and agree?"

"Yes, sir, I do."

Walker paused as he sat back in his chair and ran one hand over his jaw. He closed his eyes. Tyler smirked as he heard him mutter under his breath, "Trusting a Yankee gambler? What is the world coming to?"

Walker opened his eyes and met Tyler's.

Tyler's eyes became hard as Walker began to speak, explaining that Victoria Kelly was actually Victoria Ann McNichol, from the wealthy McNichol's of Toronto, that she was a gambler and a wild girl, raised by her father more as a man than a woman, and that her father had sent her to the west for some 'seasoning,' as he termed it.

Tyler envisioned her in pants and a form-fitting shirt, the shapely body beneath the manly exterior spoke more of the fairer sex than of any manly virtue. Her untamed, wild nature called to something inside Tyler. Something he couldn't share with Philip Walker. Something he hadn't felt in a very long time.

It excited and stirred his soul.

His thoughts were interrupted when Philip suddenly rose from behind his desk. "You must meet Anna, our maid. She was the last person in this house to see Victoria before she disappeared."

Tyler was struck by Philip's odd choice of words, 'in this house.' He filed that away for future reference.

They left the study and went into the kitchen, where Anna stood over a large wooden table in the center of the expansive kitchen, framed by sunlight streaming through tall windows that lined one wall. The room was filed with the smells of fresh baking. She was busy rolling pale white-floured dough with a rolling pin. Tyler detected the scent of cooking apples coming from the direction of a black cast iron stove in one corner of the room. There was bowl of freshly peeled apples near her on the flour-covered table. Anna looked up and smiled broadly as the two men entered, wiping her hands on the apron that covered her dress. Some of the flour had spilled onto her arms, and the contrast of the white flour against her dusky skin was striking.

Tyler broke into an easy grin as he moved toward the table. He met Anna's bright eyes and smiled.

"Anna," began Philip, "this is Mr. Scott."

Tyler nodded at the maid who smiled briefly at him again, then looked back at her employer, waiting for him to continue.

"He's going to find Miss Victoria for us and bring her home."

Tyler cringed at Walker's attitude and manner of speech. Walker spoke slowly, carefully pronouncing each word as if he were speaking to a child or someone who was slow. Walker's demeaning attitude annoyed Tyler.

Anna remained calm and seemed to hang on Philip Walker's every word. Tyler could see her shoulders rise and he watched as she calmly smoothed her hands on her apron.

"Please tell Mr. Scott about the last time you spoke with Miss Victoria."

Anna folded her hands in front of her and relaxed her shoulders as she turned to face Tyler.

She stood tall, looking him in the eyes, but at the last moment seemed to shrink and looked at the floor. Then she took a deep breath, glanced up at Tyler and began. "Mr. Scott, I saw Miss Victoria last night as she was goin' out for a walk. Being a light and restless sleeper myself, it don't surprise me when she was up at such an hour."

"Do you recall what time it was?"

"Don' rightly know, but it musta been nearly midnight, sir, the moon being bright and all."

Tyler frowned and rubbed his chin in thought. Victoria mustn't have gone very far. Somehow he didn't imagine her in the woods that lined the road, the tall thick tress would have blocked out a good deal of the moonlight. Where could she have been going so late and in the dark?

"Thank you, Anna, I'll take it from here," Philip said, briskly dismissing her.

Anna nodded to the two men, her eyes cast downward. Burying her hands in her apron pockets, she went though through a kitchen door that led to the rear of the house.

"So what do you think?" said Philip, his voice holding a trace of urgency that hadn't been there before.

Tyler looked outside and studied the wagon ruts through the kitchen windows.

Fire in their Hearts

They ran away from the house to disappear into an opening among the tall evergreens. The wind had come up, the trees, massive branches heavy with new pine cones, swayed slowly in the breeze.

Tyler went out the back door. He wanted a closer look at the wagon ruts, and wanted to examine the tracks and the area around the side of the house. His eyes narrowed. The scent of fresh pine filled his nostrils.

It was a heady aroma, but Tyler was concentrating on something far more important—Victoria's boot-prints in the dark, brown earth that ran down the right wagon rut away from the house. She had definitely been out here last night just as Anna had said, that much was certain.

He turned to face Philip, who'd followed him outside. "I'm going to follow her tracks until I lose them," he said, smiling thinly at Philip.

Tyler didn't wait for a reply, and turned away without saying another word. He started to follow the trail of boot prints that led away from the house. He was soon out of sight of the house, surrounded by the sounds of crows and other birds calling to each other in the woods. He looked up and spotted an eagle high in the distance between the tree tops, its magnificent wings spread wide as it rode the up drafts of sun-warmed air.

Tyler followed the tracks until they stopped. He studied the area carefully, squatted down and carefully scanned the ground and the bushes around him. He looked for anything that might explain Victoria's disappearance. He looked around the area where her prints ran out and increased his search area, looking for anything out of the ordinary.

Sure enough, he found two other sets of boot prints on either side of the wagon rut.

It looked like they had been there a while because the areas had broken twigs, crushed grass, and the ground was well trampled. The footprints ended with one set behind Victoria's and one in front. Both made by the same kind of boot. A western boot. The impressions also suggested the owners were wearing spurs, which meant horses. But there weren't any fresh horse tracks nearby, so the riders probably carried Victoria to where horses waited for them.

This suggested it was well planned, a possible kidnapping. A woman like Victoria wouldn't just let herself get carried away without a struggle—if she'd been conscious.

This isn't good. Though it did confirm Tyler's suspicion—and Philip's admission—that Victoria was far more than what she said she was. She was valuable to someone.

He stood still to listen to the sound of the breeze moving through the trees and the calls of the birds around him. No sounds of civilization penetrated this raw, virgin wilderness.

He slipped one hand in his trouser pocket as he studied the tracks in the soft earth. There were the three sets, but one made a deeper impression in the yielding, soft soil than the others. He kicked a small stone with his shoe, sending it airborne in the direction the prints disappeared in the forest. *What was happening on the other side of those trees?*

Tyler moved off the road, making his way deeper into the woods, following the crushed path through the undergrowth to the base of some trees where the moss had been disturbed. He squatted, resting on his haunches in order to study the shredded lichen that covered the moist forest floor more closely. Horseshoes had torn the moss as if it were paper, and crushed the ferns and salal.

He thought the two kidnappers must have tied their horses to the trees while they waited until Victoria appeared on the wagon path. *But how did they know she was going to come out at that hour, or at all?*

He stood, wiped his hands on his pant legs, then moved deeper into the woods. There was evidence of a campfire here. The gray-black ashes were still soft, powdery.

They'd been waiting for her, that much was fairly certain.

Something was definitely wrong with this picture, something that made Tyler frown. Someone who knew her true identity was behind her disappearance. The question now was who else knew her real name besides the Walkers? If he was going to save her he needed to find the *real* reason for her being in Vancouver. She wasn't here just to play poker, that much was certain.

He also felt an odd twinge, a real fear for Victoria that made his gut twist. He shook off the feeling, pushed it back in his mind, and started back for the house.

Nine

TYLER AND HANK left the Walker house with Hank driving the wagon along the narrow dirt road as they made their way back to town. In Vancouver, the makeshift tents were already beginning to give way to rough buildings. Tyler was impressed. It had only been a day since the fire had ripped through town, destroying everything.

But these were hardy people, used to making their own way in this challenging wilderness. There was certainly enough lumber around to build all the houses they needed, and he was sure that the sawmills would welcome the business.

"How long have you lived here, Hank?" Tyler asked as the wagon bounced sharply over another bump, causing his question to stutter out from between clenched teeth.

"Since the town was founded, about fifteen years ago."

"A founding father? Good for you."

Hank said nothing, just flicked the leather reins to urge the horses forward. The horses' leisurely pace gave Tyler time to think of his own home. His father had bred horses. Unfortunately, his father had been a cruel, miserable man who fought with everyone, or his horses would have been champions.

Fire in their Hearts

Tyler's mother died giving birth to him, so after his father died the horse farm automatically went to him. But Tyler had no interest in farming. Instead, he sold the farm and began his journey through the gambling parlors, losing some and winning some until he'd mastered the various card games that were played for money.

His luck was running a little thin right now, but he knew once he was behind the poker table with a sizable stake, fortune would smile on him again. Then maybe he'd be able to finally doff these itchy clothes Hank had lent him. He scratched his left arm.

The two men rode in silence until they arrived at the hotel. Emily Smart stood on the porch, a white apron over her gray skirt. Some of her blonde hair had come loose from the tight bun and tendrils of hair were playing around her face and shoulders. Her gray eyes betrayed her concern as did her restless hands as she continually smoothed her apron over and over.

"Hank," she said, rushing down the stairs to the side of the wagon as Hank dragged hard on the reins. "I heard the news. Parson Sloan stopped by and told me about Victoria. Who would do such a thing?" Emily asked, clearly distraught.

Tyler's eyebrows arched in surprise like two black arrows. *News must travel fast in small towns.*

As Hank and Tyler climbed down from the wagon, the seat squeaked in protest. Creaking wagons loaded to the brim with building supplies rolled down the street around them. Men and boys nodding grimly as they passed each other. Women called out for youngsters, who were trying to find treasure in the destroyed buildings. Tyler walked around the wagon until he stood beside Hank.

"Don't know, Em, but Mr. Scott here is gonna help us find her."

A boy approached them. He wore a loose plaid shirt and worn suspenders holding up rolled pants, which were obviously too big for him. The boy's clothing was no doubt hand-me downs from an older sibling. He had a piece of paper gripped in one grimy hand. His face and clothing were darkened by soot. "You Walker? I've a message for ya," he said as Tyler nodded.

Holding out the folded paper to Tyler, the boy gave it to him then reversed direction and headed off. "Don't you want a coin for your trouble, lad?" called Tyler after him.

"Already been paid." The echo of the boy's reply was barely heard among the noise and confusion on the street, as he scurried off like some small, terrified animal.

Tyler wondered who'd paid the boy until he opened the note and read the first line. The letters were scrawled as if by a child, but no child would write such words.

Ta Mr. Walker, Victoria die unless 10,000$ de liver by 12 tomorrow to place we tell ya.

The words must have written by someone who could barely read or write, but the meaning was clear. There was a crude map drawn on the bottom half of the page. He didn't recognize the place. "Walkers sure aren't gonna be happy," he muttered. "I've got to get this to them right away."

Hank pulled the note from Tyler's hand and studied it again, his eyes settling on the map. "I know where this is," he said matter-of-factly.

"Good, because we're gonna see the chief constable right now. It's about time the law got involved, no matter what Philip Walker says." Tyler put his right hand in his pocket and gazed at the men and wagons as they moved down the dusty street, leaving powdery brown earth that drifted down to coat everything.

Fire in their Hearts

Victoria was in real trouble and he desperately needed help to get her back. Somehow he felt a twinge of responsibility. After all, she'd saved his life.

He cursed himself. He owed her. But why did she have to be so beautiful *and* such a pain in the rear-end at the same time?

***

Victoria woke to knotted muscles in her arms and legs that screamed in protest. She moaned softly as her eyes opened into narrow slits. As her vision returned she saw that the daylight was muted and she lay in an area with rocks all around her. It looked like a tunnel of some kind.

Is this what it feels like to in a tomb, to be dead? She shivered as the thought went through her mind.

The back of her head throbbed. She studied her surroundings in more detail as her eyes focused and her mind cleared. She was in a cool, dark cavern with light streaming in from an opening twenty feet away. She was startled as a drip of cool water hit her neck and made her jump.

Sharp rocks beneath her skirt pushed through her clothing like spears. Shifting her weight slightly to one side to relieve some of the pressure points helped. She realized she was tied hand and foot and there was a gag in her mouth. She was trussed up as if she were a prize steer, like the ones she'd seen in the Boston stockyards.

She attempted to spit the gag out with no success. She tried to move her legs, but felt the ropes tighten. The movement started her blood circulating again and she felt pins and needles in her arms and legs.

Where am I?

She stopped struggling and thought hard.

She recalled walking in the ruts of the wagon tracks on the road close to the Walkers home into the forest, then being startled by a man dressed like one of those outlaws in western dime novels. She recalled his sinister blue eyes as he gazed at her, and the fear that had shot through her the moment he said her name.

Her name? *How did he know my name?*

Then blackness had enveloped her and the next thing she remembered was waking up here.

She froze when she heard the sound of scraping coming from the mouth of the cave, followed by heavy footfalls.

Someone's coming.

A tall, dark shape appeared, framed by the sunlight beyond. It was a male figure, a large man wearing a ten-gallon hat. The sound of his leather boots on the hard rocky ground echoed as he entered the cave. Victoria thought about feigning unconsciousness, but she needed to know what her situation was, so the best thing to do was confront whoever this man turned out to be.

The man stopped. He nodded then turned away and hurried back to the cave entrance.

His distant shouts echoed through the cave as he told his companions she was awake. Victoria had difficulty distinguishing the exact words, but she heard the urgency in his voice *Others? How many are there?*

She heard footsteps pounding before three man-sized shapes appeared in the cave mouth.

"Well, we're awake now, are we, princess?" said a man's voice tinged with sarcasm. "Now that's its daylight we should remove them ropes and the mouth gag. Won't do ya no good to holler, Miss Victoria. There's no one 'round here for miles anyway."

Fire in their Hearts

Victoria felt rough, calloused hands against her skin as they untied the ropes around her wrists first, then the ones around her legs. Once her hands were free, she removed the gag herself, then rubbed her legs, hands, and arms to increase the circulation. She felt a weakness in her legs, though she wasn't about to let these arrogant bastards see any vulnerability in her. She wasn't like her woman friends, some helpless eastern female who needed a man to help her out of trouble.

She managed to get to her feet, then used one hand to steady herself against the damp cave wall. The time-worn stone beneath her skin felt cool and wet to the touch. The mildew and smell of stagnant water made her wince in disgust. She glared at the man who stood before her. *He must be the leader of this bunch of cutthroats.*

"Who are you?" she demanded, "and why are you holding me?"

The man's swarthy, stubble-covered face broke into an easy grin. His thumbs were hooked on his gun belt and he stood with his weight shifted over his right foot. "I thought that was obvious, Miss Victoria."

Victoria eyed the man quizzically, her right eyebrow arched up on her pale forehead. *How did he know my name? I hate not being in control.* She glared at her captor.

Pushing herself away from the wall, she willed herself to stand up by herself, only the cave swayed and twisted around her. It was as if she were some drunken sailor on shore leave. Strong hands grabbed her and steadied her before she fell. *I don't feel very well.*

The man's grin dropped away to be replaced by a frown. "Good thing 'ol Pete was behind you or you'd be lying flat on your back about now. Take it easy now, Miss Victoria, we don't want you to get hurt, your very valuable to us."

"Then you shouldn't have hit me so hard." Victoria spat the words as anger seethed from within her.

The man nodded. "Yup, your right, Miss Victoria. 'Ol Pete's just too good at what he does."

They all started to laugh. Her head throbbed harder than before as the noise bounced and echoed off the cave walls.

The cave seemed to move, rocking back and forth like a ship at sea. Strong hands on her elbows guided her to the cave mouth, then outside into the bright sunlight. She blinked away the water that filled her eyes. Everything was a blur. In a few minutes her vision cleared sufficiently for her to make out her surroundings. *We're in the mountains.*

They made their way slowly over the rough ground to a clearing where a small campfire burned. The wood crackled and smoke filled the air. *I've smelled enough burning wood to last a lifetime.*

A gray iron coffee pot rested next to the flames. Four bedrolls surrounded the fire, and three bays and one chestnut horse stood off to one side, their saddles resting on the ground near them as they watched the humans approach. So far Victoria had only seen the three men, the extra bedroll and horse meant another kidnapper was nearby.

Crows squawked to each other from the top of the tall evergreen trees overhead to split the quiet of the morning air. A breeze made the tops of the trees sway, it felt gentle on her skin.

The warm air and the sunlight seeped into her bones helping to warm and rejuvenate her, though she was still light-headed and a long way from her normal self.

Fire in their Hearts

"Why don't you take a seat next to the fire. This place is so damp compared to what we're used to," said Stubble-man, as he moved to stand beside the fire. His scuffed leather boots were testament to the many hours he'd worn them. Stubble bent down to retrieve a metal coffee cup from a bedroll. She assumed it was his.

He proceeded to use the edge of a stained, woolen blanket to grip the handle on the coffee pot then pour some of the streaming black liquid into the cup.

"You like some, Miss Victoria?" Stubble asked. He made a point of not looking at her, his hazel eyes focused on the cup.

"I don't want anything from you." Her voice filled with contempt and defiance as she looked away from him.

From behind her she heard ol' Pete's deep-throated chuckle.

Stubble shrugged his broad shoulders and squatted next to the fire, glancing at her. He took a sip of the coffee. "Told ya, she'd be a wild cat." He shook his head as he shifted his gaze to the woods to the west.

The dizziness returned. Victoria knew she had to sit down immediately before she fell down. She felt it important to maintain the illusion that she was stronger and more in control than she actually was. She gingerly moved to a log at the edge of the makeshift campsite and sat down, just in time before her knees buckled under her.

She continued to glare at the two men, who ignored her. Pete moved to his bedroll to retrieve his own tin cup. He poured himself some coffee, then stood, calmly watching her over the rim of his cup. His pale, blue eyes focused on her as if he were daring her to make a run for it. She knew with absolute certainty that she was in no condition to run anywhere, but 'ol Pete', as Stubble called him, didn't have to know that.

She stared back at him, like she used to do with Buttons, her cat, when she was a girl. Eventually she won and he averted his gaze.

Odd, it was like they were waiting for something to happen. She sensed their anxiousness. *Interesting. How can I use this?*

The silence was shattered by the sound of branches being broken in the stand of trees to the west. Someone was coming. *This must be the real leader of this gang of outlaws.* "Outlaws" was a new term coined by the eastern papers.

Stubble stood and tossed his remaining coffee into the dirt just as the tree branches separated to reveal the new arrival.

Victoria's eyes went wide as a red-haired woman, with pale skin the color of fine china, stepped into the clearing. She wore a black cotton riding skirt and a white cotton shirt with black leather riding boots. A large caliber six-gun hung off her right hip, encased in a worn, brown, leather holster. Her mane of red curls seemed to be uncontrolled, but Victoria could see the leather strap around her neck attached to her hat.

The woman nodded to the two men, then glared at Victoria. Suddenly Victoria felt as weak as a newborn kitten. She fought the sensation as blackness crept into the edge of her vision. Just before she blacked out her final thought was how could a woman could be the leader of a gang of cut throats? *What's wrong with me? A woman can do anything a man can do.*

The forest around her disappeared into a swirling vortex of vivid color at the edge of her vision. As everything went black she sagged to the ground.

***

Tyler stopped outside the canvas tent identified by the words *Vancouver Police Department* painted in crude black lettering on a makeshift sign nailed to the post in front of the tent.

Tyler couldn't see anyone inside, neither the rotund chief constable, or his 'force' of two deputies.

An older man sat outside his tent, next to the police tent, on a canvas-and-wood framed chair smoking a hand-carved pipe. A small cooking fire smoldered in a circle of smooth, gray stones near him. A tin coffee pot steamed next to the low, banked, red and blue flames. Tyler could smell the coffee from where he stood.

The old man's face was grizzled with deep age lines. White stubble covered a lean, tanned face that was the texture of fine leather. His sky blue eyes were clear as he watched Tyler from where he sat.

"Ya lookin' for someone?" the old man asked as he removed his pipe from between his pale lips. His dry, creaky voice reminded Tyler of an old door being closed.

Tyler gazed at the man at the man sitting there. "Yeah. I'm lookin' for Chief McNalley. Know where he is?"

The old man looked thoughtful for a moment. "Let's see, 'ol Cy could be just 'bout anywhere at this time 'o day." He looked up at the sky as if it were a pocket watch, which to him it probably was. "Normally he likes the bar this time 'o day, but he's been a little busy for that lately. So all I know is, he's not there. That much's for certain." He paused to scratch his stubbled narrow chin. "Naw, he's probably gone somewhere with Diller."

"You don't know where Diller is, do you?" said Tyler.

"Nope," said the old man, with a twinkle in his eyes. He leaned back in his chair, put his pipe back between his lips, and tried to puff on it. But it must have gone out, because he stuck a long, thin stick into the flames, got a spark, then lifted it to the bowl of his pipe and re-lit the tobacco inside with two puffs.

102

Tyler smiled thinly and nodded. *The old man's wasting my time on purpose. I wonder why?*

Tyler turned and headed down the dusty street, passing more tents. Inside some were women nursing babies. Still other women were chasing toddlers about, herding them like miniature cattle on a stampede. The air was pungent with cooking odors as women prepared meals in large, coal black pots hung on steel bars over open fire pits.

It struck Tyler as an ironic twist that sometimes fire was your mortal enemy, while at other times a valuable friend.

Finally he came upon a group of men busy nailing boards across the frame of a building. Rebuilding a store front.

"Excuse me, gentlemen."

One of the men stopped hammering and looked up, his dark blue, red-rimmed, tired eyes flat, betraying no emotion. "What can we do for ya?"

"I'm lookin' for Chief McNalley."

"He's at Diller's place—one street over, three tents down."

Tyler was startled yet pleased to discover that the old man was right. *He hadn't lied to me.* Guys like McNalley were just too predictable.

"Thanks," he said. The man nodded in reply then went back to work.

As instructed, Tyler made his way between the tents and to the third one from the end. Sure enough, there, seated just inside the tent flap were the two men. Mayor Diller sat across from Chief McNalley in front of an oak barrel they were using as a table. They each held a glass half-filled with a brownish-orange liquid Tyler assumed was whiskey.

Even if they offered, which was unlikely, he thought it would be better for him to ignore the liquor. He needed his wits clear and their help if he was going to rescue Victoria.

"I'm glad I found you two gentlemen. I need your help," Tyler said, with a trace of a sigh in his voice.

The two men gazed up at him as if he'd lost his mind by interrupting them. McNalley frowned. He took a sip of whiskey from his glass, then said, "Mr. Scott, I'd advise you to make yourself scarce at the moment. The Mayor and I are discussing important city business."

Tyler continued, ignoring McNalley. "Miss Kelly's been kidnapped and Mr. Walker has been sent a ransom note." Tyler wasn't about to reveal his suspicions about Victoria's last name being an alias. He decided that he was going to hold onto that piece of information for awhile and not show them his hold card. At least not yet. Besides one or both of these men might be involved.

As his father used to tell him, *"Never trust anyone until they've proven themselves,"*—advice that had saved him considerable grief many times during his travels around the continent, especially in his chosen profession.

Being a gambler meant you could meet up with the most unsavory characters. Many cutthroats and cowboys would kill you without the slightest provocation. That was why he'd taken to carrying a Bowie knife strapped to his right leg, and a black-barreled, walnut-handled derringer hidden inside the sleeve of his coat. The derringer was secured to a spring loaded ejector that thrust the weapon into his right hand should he ever need it. It only fired two shots, but it had proven itself a sufficient deterrent to drunken cowboys who discovered they were lousy card players.

Tyler had also learned to pace his liquor consumption to keep his mind sharp. The knife made an excellent backup for those awkward moments when the friends of said drunken cowboy came at him after he'd staved off the initial unwelcome advance.

Unfortunately, he only had his knife with him at the moment, due to the fire. But he was determined to obtain another derringer or other suitable weaponry before he went charging off to the rescue of the damsel in distress. He winced at that thought. *I'm a card player, not a hero. Besides heroes die young and I want to live to a very ripe old age.*

The chief constable stared back at him, his watery eyes and reddish complexion outwardly calm. He took a large sip of the whiskey then set the glass on top of the makeshift table. "Kidnapped? When? By whom?" the large man said, his speech slurred.

Before Tyler could reply the mayor entered the conversation. "Who around here would do such a thing?" He sounded indignant and a little drunk, too. Tyler knew he'd better be careful. He couldn't pull off this rescue single-handedly. The way the kidnapping had been done told him he was dealing with pros. Probably guns for hire. And he wasn't about to trust these men, at least not yet. For all he knew, they may even be involved in this.

Someone who was close to Victoria and knew her habits had betrayed her. Until he was satisfied, everyone was a suspect.

"Frankly, gentlemen, I really don't know, but I'm determined to find out and rescue her."

McNalley snorted loudly, the ends of his long, greasy mustache whipping about like two snakes on the end of a tether. "What a load of horse-hooey. Why don't Mr. Walker just pay the ransom and that'll be that?"

Tyler's dark eyes flared, but he maintained his outward calm. He struggled to keep his emotions in check. *Is this "sworn officer of the law" a complete fool?*

Tyler sensed time was short, he needed to get a rescue party together now.

"Well then, Chief Constable, I guess I'm on my own," Tyler turned and started to walk away, when he heard a gruff voice call his name. He stopped and turned back, finding himself face-to-face with both the chief constable and the mayor. McNalley stood, his arms like tree trunks crossed over his massive chest, his gaze intense. "I don't want no American messing 'round in my jurisdiction. I'll ask one of my deputies to meet you at your hotel in, say, an hour. He'll assist you with your investigation. And we better not catch you with any guns, Mr. Scott, or you'll end up in my jail." He paused, his eyes doubtful as he looked at the tent. "When I have one."

Babysit me, is more like it. A slow grin crossed Tyler's dark features. He nodded. "Thank you, Chief Constable. I'll expect him in an hour."

Tyler headed for the Brighton Hotel. The hour would give him time to buy a gun with some of his stake money. Though he hated to dip into his precious stake, his instincts told him he'd need some firepower if he and Victoria were going to get out of this mess alive.

Ten

PRECISELY AN HOUR later, a young man in a woolen policeman's uniform showed up in the lobby of the Brighton Hotel asking for Tyler Scott. While he'd waited, Tyler had managed to secure a Colt Peacemaker from a peddler who happened to have an extra among the wide variety of items he offered for sale.

Tyler had hidden the revolver in the small of his back beneath his jacket in the waistband of his pants. He hoped the lump wouldn't show too much.

The constable, a youngish man with a freckled face and carrot orange hair, looked more like twelve than his true age of twenty-two. He smiled warmly at Tyler. His sea green eyes sparkled as if the sun danced off them as he watched Tyler come down the staircase.

"Constable James Nelson," he said, "you must be Tyler Scott." They shook hands and Tyler felt the boy's firm grip. He was confident, that much was certain.

Tyler grinned at the young man. "Ya, I'm Tyler Scott. Call me Ty."

Nelson grinned. Tyler immediately liked this young man.

"Of course, Ty, and please call me Jim. That's what my friends call me."

Tyler's eyebrows went up in surprise. "You're a friendly fella. I thought—"

Jim chuckled. "Don't worry. I'm here to help you find the young lady, not just to spy for the chief constable. His nose is out'a joint because Mr. Walker asked you to find Miss Victoria before he asked the chief, that's his problem not mine. I can assure you, I'm here to help, not to hinder."

Tyler rested one hand on Jim's right shoulder. "Well then, Jim, I guess we're in this together." Jim nodded.

"I've got two horses saddled and provisioned outside so we can get started right away if you'd like."

"Yes, of course," Tyler patted his money belt and thought for a second he might place it in the hotel safe, then shrugged inwardly and decided to carry the money with him just in case. First things first, though, before they left.

"You go outside. I'll meet up with you in a moment," Tyler said.

Jim nodded, turned, and went out the front door. A small bell now hung over the door and it tinkled brightly as the door closed behind the young constable.

Tyler reached into the inside pocket of his jacket and pulled out two envelopes. On one of them was the name Philip Walker, the other was blank. He didn't know if the envelope he'd made out for the kidnappers was going to get to them in time, but he suspected that if he left it on the lobby reception desk it would somehow fall into their hands.

He placed both envelopes carefully on the desk, glanced about the empty lobby, then walked out the front door into the street.

"We need to make one more stop." Tyler paused and glanced at the young constable. "Do you think you can get another horse?"

"Sure." Jim shrugged and gave Tyler a wide grin.

"Good enough," said Tyler with a smile. "Com'on."

Tyler led the constable to the rear of the Brighton Hotel and entered the barroom. The card players were gone and Willie stood leaning on the bar. He was reading a newspaper, the pages open on the polished surface. Willie glanced up at the new arrivals, a slow smile spread across his dusky features as he saw the young constable in his ill-fitting blue woolen uniform trailing behind Tyler.

Willie raised one eyebrow in the direction of the constable. "What you bringin' 'im in here for?"

Tyler chuckled. "Don't worry, Willie, me and young Jim here are on a mission. And I was wonderin' if you'd be willing to join us?"

The bartender raised his elbows off the bar and stood straight, raising his tree-trunk-like frame to its full six-foot-plus height. "Mission?"

Tyler could see the flash of interest in Willie's eyes as curiosity oozed from his every pore. He decided to let him know who they were rescuing. If they were going to die, they should know who they were dying for.

"Yup, a rescue mission. Miss Victoria McNichol has been kidnapped, me and Jim here plan to go after her. Thought maybe you might be willing to help. I could use a man handy with a shotgun. "Tyler eyed the bartender. "You know, in case we run into a little trouble."

Willie eyes remained fixed on Tyler's as he considered the gambler's words. "I thought her name was Kelly, Victoria Kelly."

Tyler nodded. "So did I, until Philip Walker told me otherwise."

Both of Willie's black eyebrows arched on his dark forehead at this news. "Really?" He rubbed the tip of his narrow chin. "This is getting interesting." Tyler waited, he could see Willie had made his decision when he nodded. "Okay, Mr. Scott, I'm with ya."

"Call me Ty, okay?"

Willie nodded.

"You still got my winnings from the game the other day?"

Willie nodded again.

"Good. Get it and let's do some shopping. We'll need more firepower if we're gonna pull this thing off."

Until now Jim Nelson had remained a silent observer of the conversation between the two men. "Uh...Mr. Scott...huh...Ty, you can't just go off buying guns. It's illegal to carry firearms in this country."

Tyler placed one large hand on the constable's chest and pressed lightly. "Don't tell me, you guys walk around unarmed?"

Jim nodded, his eyes grew large and he bit his lower lip as his expression reflected his concern.

"I didn't say you have to carry a gun. All I know is, if I'm gonna go up against armed kidnappers, which they most certainly will be, then I'm going to be carrying a Peacemaker," Tyler spoke with firm conviction.

Jim's face paled and he swallowed hard. "You really think they'll be armed?"

Tyler nodded and glanced at Willie, who gave him a sardonic grin as he reached below the bar to retrieve his shotgun. He hefted the weapon to a cradle position in his arms.

"Well, in that case maybe we all better be carrying some protection," said Jim.

Tyler and Willie laughed as Tyler slipped one arm around the pale-faced, young policeman's shoulder. Together the three men headed for the door.

***

The trio of would be rescuers arrived at the makeshift livery stable that was filling in for the original structure destroyed in the fire.

On the way to the stable Jim told them about a blacksmith who was relatively new to the province and might be willing to join them.

The blacksmith hailed from Montana, and he'd been a little evasive about his previous occupation since arriving in Vancouver. His name was Harcourt Sims, though he preferred to be called Harry, the blacksmith.

Entering the stable, they paused to eye the horses tethered to the row of wooden posts pounded into the soft earth with sufficient force to ensure no horse this side of Texas would be able to pry themselves loose. A booming voice from behind a stand of pine trees in the neighboring forest cut through the air, ordering them to the western side of the stable enclosure.

"What do you three think you're doin' here?" The voice rang out again as a barrel-chested man, with hair the color of red clay, stepped from the forest, broad-handled axe gripped in one massive hand. His chest was bare and glistened with perspiration. His bushy red eyebrows formed a V over intense green eyes.

Tyler took a deep breath, smiled easily, and walked toward the man heading for him with the axe now resting over his shoulder. As the giant moved, Tyler could see his rippling muscles. He knew he would need all his powers of persuasion to convince this mountain of a man to join and help them.

111

"Sorry, friend, we're just looking for some horses for hire, that's all." Tyler spoke with a calm steady voice.

The man stood towering over him now with one eyebrow arched in query, his sharp eyes wary as he studied the smaller man standing in front of him. His easy stance said he could just as easily part Tyler like a cedar right down the middle with the axe he carried.

"None 'o those are for hire or sale." The giant motioned him away with a flick of his hand as if Tyler were a fly buzzing about his head bothering him.

"A woman's been kidnapped and we mean to rescue her," said Tyler. His voice was edged with foreboding, his expression calm.

The giant stopped short, his mouth agape. He stared at the smaller man, his ruddy features registered his surprise.

Tyler suspected the big man usually got his way in most situations. The giant eyed Tyler closely as he moved toward the gambler. He came close enough that Tyler could feel the man's hot breath, reeking of stale tobacco, wash over him.

"You got balls, boy." His hard features suddenly brightened as a wide grin split his face. He stepped back. "I like that. Most men are so feared o' me they wouldn't dare challenge me. Course I could easily snap you like a twig, but I don't cotton to such things. Wouldn't be very Christian of me now, would it?"

Tyler didn't move, he just stood there and nodded.

"The name's Sims. So how many horses did you say you needed?"

Tyler glanced at his two companions who stood stock still watching the interaction between the two men. Willie's dark skin actually looked as if it had gone a shade paler. Both men's eyes were wide as saucers.

Tyler turned to look at Sims, and a half-smile crossed his rugged features. "You interested in a job, Mr. Sims?"

Within the hour four riders, each astride a horse, rode down Hastings Street headed for the forest surrounding Philip Walker's house on the edge of town.

Eleven

"NAME'S ARMSTRONG, Miles Armstrong, ma'am. From Utah." The cowboy sat across from Victoria on a log next to the low-burning fire. The acrid, white smoke drifted upward to be lost in the sky overhead. Victoria hoped someone could see the smoke before it could dissipate.

"Sorry for the trouble, ma'am, but we got a job ta..."

"Shut up, Miles," snapped a female voice from behind Victoria. "You don't have the education or breeding to be speaking to the high and mighty, Victoria Ann McNichol."

Victoria whirled to see the red-haired woman glaring at her. The woman's cold green eyes seemed to bore through Victoria.

Victoria had recovered from her fainting spell and was now seated on a log next to the fire that had burned itself down to red embers.

Who is this woman? She certainly seemed to know Victoria's real name. The straight ahead approach always seems to work best in situations like this. Victoria winced. *When have I ever been in a situation like this before?*

"Who are you?" Victoria said, her mouth firm, her eyes brimming with contempt.

The woman smiled, like a sly fox, closed-mouthed and confident. "You really think I'd tell you anything?" She turned away from Victoria. Her long hair hung down over her back, a dark red mane of curls.

She said something softly to Armstrong, her unshaven cohort, who nodded. The breeze was blowing from behind her and Victoria could only make out every second word. Even with that limited information she was certain that her time on this earth was short.

Victoria wasn't used to being treated with such disregard but held her temper in check. She knew this woman wasn't to be trifled with, and very likely a match for her in every way she could think of. What really bothered Victoria was who this gang was ultimately working for. Who had the money to hire them? Most importantly, who knew who she was—and did they know why she was in Vancouver?

The woman spoke with a slight accent. Her word usage indicated she was better educated than the men who worked for her. The accent bothered Victoria. *Where have I heard it before?* She scanned her memory but the inflection in the woman's voice escaped her.

"At least tell me your name," said Victoria.

The woman turned to face Victoria, her eyes getting larger with surprise then narrowing again as she smirked. Victoria felt a sense of victory for the first time since she'd woken up in the cave.

"Rose— my name is Rose, if you must know— and that's all you need for now." She turned away and began issuing orders to her band of outlaws. "Put out the campfire and prepare the horses."

Victoria suspected they needed to move to stay one step ahead of any would-be rescuers. Once her orders spurred the men into action, Rose glanced back at Victoria.

"And Pete, hog-tie Miss Victoria here and put her over your horse. You're going to be responsible for her, understand?"

"Yes, ma'am." The large cowboy nervously licked his lips. He looked afraid of this woman. Victoria wondered how Rose held these men under her thumb. What power did she have over them? It wouldn't be a bad idea to find out—and could be useful in the future. *If I make it out of here alive, that is.*

Pete turned, hitching up his gun belt with one hand as he walked toward her, gripping a length of coarse rope in his massive hand. Victoria sighed and knew that it was useless to fight him. This wasn't going to be the most comfortable ride she'd ever experienced, that much was certain, and Pete didn't look like the soft, gentle type.

***

Tyler and his three companions stood over the burned-out campfire they found next to the mountain cave.

The dirt was blackened from the fire the kidnappers had used to keep them warm while they waited for their opportunity to kidnap Victoria. No doubt the fire had only been lit during the day, so as not to alert anyone they were there. The smoke would be lost in the winds that constantly moved the trees. The air smelled of the tall pines and firs of the forest that even now swayed in the strong breeze. The scent of the trees mingled with the pungent odor of damp, rotting groundcover that never managed to get any sunlight beneath the boughs of the massive trees.

Tyler's gaze focused on the immediate area surrounding the fire pit, looking for tracks. Sure enough, there were four sets of boot prints and four sets of hoof-prints depressed in the soft ground. The tracks led off to the west, and were deeper as they moved farther away form the campfire.

"They went this way," Tyler said, following the tracks. In his hands he held the reins of the bay stallion Harry had supplied him with. He walked as he led the horse among the trees. It was a sturdy animal, which was a good thing since they might have to travel some distance to catch up with the kidnappers. The three men followed Tyler until they came to a clearing, each walking alongside their horses. The closeness of the trees and the tangled underbrush made navigating on horseback difficult.

At the edge of the clearing was an open area leading west toward a point that jutted out from the mainland into theP coast. Tyler had come to Vancouver on a cargo ship that sailed from Seattle and he'd seen this jut of land from the sea. It was rugged, strewn with boulders and high unassailable cliffs.

No doubt there were caves that dotted the area, which would be just the place for the kidnappers to hide out. It would be the kind of place he'd choose, if he were planning something like this.

The four mounted their horses and headed west toward the ocean. The air smelled of salt from the Pacific Ocean. Once they were out from under the shadow of the trees, the sunshine felt warm on their faces. Gray and white seagulls cried out to each other high overhead as they swooped and danced in the summer air.

Soon they were high on a cliff overlooking the bay. The blue-green water below was dotted with foaming whitecaps until it met the sandy shore. The bay was wide, at least three or four miles across, with green rolling hills on the opposite side. The hills mirrored the waves until they met the side of the mountain range that towered above them to the south. Some of the highest peaks were still blanketed with snow, being so tall that the sunshine was ineffective in making the snow and ice fully melt even in summer.

"Anyone know this area?" Tyler looked at his companions.

Young Jim shook his head. "I only arrived here a month ago from Seattle myself. Boston originally."

Tyler smiled to himself. *Is everyone from Boston?*

"Don't pay me to come out here," said Willie in a matter-of-fact way. Tyler knew what he meant. A black man alone in these parts took his life in his hands if he ventured outside the confines of the city. Travel was still a risky thing even for a white man.

"I know it some," said Harry. "I've taken some of the finer folk riding out here so they could see the ocean from the tip of the point. On a clear day you can see Vancouver Island."

Tyler smirked. *Figures.* Harry seemed like the enterprising type. "Okay, Harry, so what's down this ridge?" He pointed to the ridge below them, which had a sharp drop off to the rocky beach far below.

"Well, as I recall, there's a lot of caves down there in the hillside. Too steep though. No way could a horse be rode down there."

Tyler nodded. "All right, where do you think is the best place to hide out around here?"

Harry looked thoughtful, his eyes going over the land in front of him, his hands resting on the horn of his saddle. The black stallion's long tail swished the flies away as it stood calmly waiting for the blacksmith's instructions. Finally Harry said, "Heading north there's some small hills a short way into the forest, and a few caves. That's where I'd be goin'."

Tyler grinned at Willie, who shrugged, then at Jim, who looked eager to go. The young constable seemed to be warming to the idea of giving chase. Tyler knew that the most difficult part of their rescue mission was yet to come.

What would they do when they came upon the kidnappers? There was going to be a shoot-out, that much was certain, and very likely deaths. The only real question now was who would die and who would live?

Harry pulled firmly on the reins of his horse to turn the animal to the southwest, Tyler, Willie, and Jim following him as they began the arduous trek inland. The nest of trees and undergrowth ahead— smaller bushes growing thick amongst the tall dark fir trees—would make the ride challenging. They would first need to get through a valley choked with underbrush if they were going to cover the ground to the caves in a reasonable time. They'd been riding all afternoon and Tyler could tell the horses were tiring. They'd need to find a spot to camp and rest up before they tackled the valley first thing in the morning.

***

The four men sat quietly around the campfire, every man's face drawn with exhaustion. They had managed to cut their way through the heavy underbrush; it had been an arduous task that took its toll on the men. It seemed every muscle in Tyler's body was aching, especially in his back and legs.

They'd enjoyed the meal of beans, bacon, and biscuits Willie made for them.

Tyler chewed slowly, gazing upward at the brilliant star-covered sky. They twinkled brightly at him. There was no moon yet, but it would be up soon. The sky would occasionally brighten as a shooting star flashed across.

When he was child he'd been told those were angels returning to Earth to do good deeds for those who prayed. He'd never had an anything like an angel visit him until he'd seen Victoria's gentle features.

Her flawless skin and creamy complexion was like an angel. At least, what he thought an angel might look like.

"There's something we need to talk about," Tyler said, his low voice filled with fatigue.

The three men, sitting on logs they'd dragged near the fire, regarded him, all of them expectant. The evening had become cool now, moths and bugs swooped and dove over the flames, drawn to the warmth and light.

Tyler focused his dark eyes on the dancing flames, watching the moths until he shifted his gaze to study the faces of his weary posse. "These kidnappers will very likely be heavily armed and experienced gunfighters. I have no doubt that we'll be in for a real fight once we catch up to them." He paused and drew in a deep breath. "If any of you wish to turn back now I'll think no less of you. As for me, I am going on alone if needed. Not for any money, but because I owe Victoria my life."

He shifted his gaze to the star-filled sky overhead. "None of you have to choose right now. In the morning, after we've had some rest and you've given it some thought, you can each let me know your decision. I figure we've got about seven hours till daybreak. I'll take first watch and wake one of you in a couple of hours to take my place."

The men nodded, dropped their bedrolls next to the fire, and curled up. Soon the sound of snores drowned out the crickets and other night creatures surrounding them. Tyler sat watching the fire, uncertain what the future held for them.

***

As the sun crept up and broke over the eastern horizon Tyler felt a gentle nudge against his side.

He rubbed sleep from his eyes with the heel of his hands, looking up he saw the red-tinged grin of Harry, who was bent over him.

"Is it time?" Tyler asked, his speech slow and slurred, his mouth dry.

"Yup, horses are saddled and ready ta go. Willie's got us some cold biscuits and bacon we can eat on the way. Coffee's ready, it's hot and thick," Harry's voice betrayed his dislike for the fare, but they had little choice of cuisine at the moment.

What Tyler wouldn't give for a fire-grilled steak and real eggs right now. *Oh well, no use thinking about it.*

He sat up and ran his hands through his dark, wavy hair. He rubbed his eyes again to shake the sleep off. He didn't feel fully refreshed, but he did feel slightly better than when he managed to drop off a couple of hours ago, after Harry had relieved him.

Tyler rolled up his bedroll and tied it behind his horse's saddle. He pulled off the leather canteen and took a large swig of water, then poured some over his face, shivering as the cool water ran down his neck and shirt. It would soon dry under the warmth of the sun.

With each passing moment the yellow ball of the sun grew higher in the blue sky spreading its fingers of warmth over the clearing where they'd bedded down. Their fire had gone out long ago. All that was left was a pile of ash surrounded by blackened stones.

Willie came up to him with a tin coffee cup in one hand and handed it to him. "I saved you a cup, Ty." The bartender smiled slightly, then nodded as Tyler took the cup and smiled back at him. He took a big gulp then nodded to Willie. The bartender turned and headed for his own bay.

Fire in their Hearts

With practiced ease, Willie stepped up into the stirrup and heaved himself into the saddle. Jim was already on his own horse watching them, looking as eager to get going as he had the day before. Tyler remembered what it was like, being the eager young man yearning for adventure. That was a long time ago. Over the years the road and lean times had quenched the youthful enthusiasm he'd once had. Though he wasn't an old man by any stretch of the imagination, he sometimes felt far beyond his thirty-one years. Tyler was certain that in many ways he had not only become older, but hopefully wiser, too.

Tyler looked into the expectant faces of the men surrounding him as he sipped some more of the coffee. It tasted bitter and yet somehow satisfying. They were about to do something significant, it felt right.

He finished his coffee and mounted.

There was no breeze, no bird call, the silence around them was like the calm before the storm.

"So who's riding with me today?"

"We discussed the matter amongst ourselves some while you was sleeping, and decided we're all with you," said Harry, his deep voice sounding louder than usual in the still air.

Tyler looked into each man's eyes and they nodded. The look of sheer determination was also there. These men had a fire in their bellies and in their hearts.

"Okay, then, let's get going and find Victoria. We need to do some rescuing!"

Tyler turned his horse and started off toward the forest, confident they could pull this off. The gang who took Victoria would regret this day, of that he had no doubt.

***

Victoria was dropped from the back of the horse onto the hard ground, her legs and hands raw from the rough rope that secured her. Pete had carried her across his lap in the saddle like so much baggage. Every muscle in her body screamed with pain from the bouncing ride across the difficult terrain. The landscape was angled toward the sea. She could hear sea gulls, the pounding surf beyond the trees, and smell salt in the air. The ground was strewn with boulders and pale yellow grass that rose to the knees of the horse. She knew because she had a good look at the ground underneath the horse's belly from her vantage point across Pete's saddle.

They had ridden for such a long time, finally after what seemed like an eternity they stopped. She was dropped from the horse and landed on her bottom in the grass with a muffled thump. A startled brown-striped snake slid over her right hand and a scream bubbled up inside of her, but she managed to suppress it. Before leaving home, her father had told her the snakes in this part of the country were harmless, except the rattlesnakes. Regardless, she detested the slimy, filthy reptiles in spite of the fact that her sudden arrival had probably terrified it.

Meanwhile Pete and his comrades had dismounted, walked a short distance away, and were standing about speaking in low tones. Their leader strode toward Victoria, swinging a long-bladed knife in her left hand. Victoria looked at the blade and realized that she couldn't take her eyes from the glinting, cold steel. Rose looked at Victoria with a cold smile that sent a chill up Victoria's spine, twisting the knife in the air so Victoria could see what she had in her hand. Her eyes flashed with an arrogance that Victoria wanted so badly to wipe off her face. Victoria felt her heart start to beat hard and her lips pursed together as she felt her fear turning to anger.

123

Her time will come.

"So how's our little princess?" said Rose as she stopped and bent over to cut the ropes binding Victoria's feet and hands together. She chuckled lightly as she stepped back and sheathed the large knife in the belt on her skirt.

Victoria glared silently at her captor and began to rub her wrists. Her legs felt weak and tingled sharply as the circulation returned. She was afraid that she'd fall if she stood too quickly, so she remained seated among the tall yellow grass. Rose turned her back to Victoria and went back to her men.

Finally Victoria felt ready and managed to gain her feet. She took one careful step forward as her head begin to swim. She took a deep breath, closing her eyes until the world steadied itself. Finally she opened her eyes to see the men laughing and pointing at her. Rose was watching her, too, with a satisfied smile on her face.

"Little princess not feeling so well?" asked Rose, in a loud mocking tone.

Victoria slowly shuffled over to a log and sat down. Black spots were still dancing in front of her eyes. "What have you got against me?" she asked Rose. She'd finally been pushed hard enough by this woman. Given the way she felt right now, she didn't care what they did to her.

Rose calmly strolled toward her until she stood over Victoria, her hands clenched into tight fists that rested on her narrow hips. "I'm sick and tired of being looked down upon by *your* type. I've spent enough time being spat on by you upper-crust spoiled brats. I'm gonna get enough of a reward for this job that I'll be able to buy my way into respectability and leave this dusty trail behind. He promised me…" Rose suddenly stopped, as if realizing she was saying too much.

Victoria started and looked into the woman's eyes. For the first time the arrogant confidence she saw in Rose faded. *'He'? Who was this 'he'?*

Rose shook her head, snorted in disgust as she turned to walk away, leaving Victoria alone.

"Don't forget to tie the princess up, nice and tight. And the gag, don't forget that either." Rose instructed the men as she returned to them.

***

Willie rested his upper body on his elbows as he lay on his belly in the tall grass waiting to catch sight of the kidnappers. He held a pair of scuffed Civil War field glasses Tyler had procured and focused on the depression in the low, rolling hills that lay before him. He glanced over and watched the horses shift uneasily as their long tails swished away the flies that hovered around them like a boiling cloud.

Looking back at the depression he saw the two men, one thin with a narrow face and gray stubble on his face, the other much bigger, with a large pot belly hanging over his gun belt. Both men wore six-guns in leather holsters, and each had a carbine resting across their laps. They sat around a small campfire with a steel coffee pot smoldering beside it. The trail of white smoke from the low flame drifted upward to be caught and carried into the cloudless sky.

He couldn't see anyone else at the camp site, but the presence of four horses told him he was looking for at least four kidnappers. He also didn't see Victoria anywhere within his line of sight. There was a slight rise to one side of the hills that he couldn't see over, so he surmised the rest were on the other side. The two below him seemed to be waiting.

Fire in their Hearts

Harry had said these grass-covered hills were the most likely place were they would find the gang. Willie smelled smoke before he saw them, and managed to find a good lookout point from above where they couldn't see him. The horses stirred slightly as he stopped in front of three pairs of expectant eyes.

The smell of sweet, crushed grass surrounded him as he crawled back down the bank until he was well out of sight and able to get to his feet. He hurried back to his gathered comrades, who waited for his report. They'd very likely have ran smack into the middle of the gang if Harry hadn't suggested he should scout ahead.

"I only saw two of 'em. Not the girl or the other two, though," Willie said breathlessly. "But all four horses were there."

Tyler rubbed his stubble-covered chin with his right hand and his dark eyes narrowed. Willie had been right when they counted the number of horse tracks. He'd hoped they were attempting a ruse by trying to appear as if they were more than they actually were. Nope there were five all right, including Victoria.

"I say we take out those two and then find the others," said Harry, who'd been itching for a fight all morning.

"Can't risk it," said Tyler. "They might kill the girl if we move too soon. Willie, you take young James here with you and circle around behind them. We need to know where every one of them is before we make our move."

Jim winced at the reference to his youth and Tyler gave him a half grin. Jim grinned back.

"And, Harry, let's make sure we take at least one prisoner. I want to find out who's behind all this," Tyler said.

The big blacksmith stopped, stared at Tyler. Harry pursed his lips in annoyance, looking disappointed, but nodded and started up the ridge, his giant strides forcing Tyler to run to keep up.

Tyler glanced over his shoulder and saw Willie, followed by Jim, who'd removed his dark blue uniform jacket to reveal a plain white cotton shirt beneath that would make it easier for him to hide in the tall grass. They headed west, away from their previous position. Tyler knew they would circle around behind the second row of hills to try to spot the absent members of the gang and to see if Victoria was with them.

As Tyler reached the crest of the hilltop he lay flat in the grass and crawled on his belly until he could see Harry's scuffed tan leather boots ahead of him. He had a pair of binoculars, too, which he brought up to his eyes as he came into position beside Harry.

Harry pointed down the side of the hill and, sure enough, there were the two men, just as Willie had described, seated on logs by a fire. Four horses were tied to a log off to their left. They seemed to be arguing, and weren't focused on the horses, which gave Tyler an idea.

He tapped Harry on the shoulder. Harry dropped Willie's field glasses and frowned down at Tyler. Tyler signaled that they needed to retreat down the hill. Harry nodded as he turned to crawl back to the base of the hill.

Tyler stood up and brushed the accumulated dirt off his pants. "I have a plan," he said.

Harry's eyes lit up and he grinned.

**

Two hours later, after Jim and Willie returned from their scouting mission, the men sat down to listen to Tyler's plan. Once he'd laid out what he wanted to do, there were knowing smiles exchanged all around. They would have to spilt up into two groups again to put the plan into action.

Tyler didn't like the idea of the splitting up.

Fire in their Hearts

He couldn't help but feel the bad guys were winning this battle before it had been fought. The old saying 'divide and conquer' came to mind. He shook away the thoughts.

This time Willie, with his shotgun, and Jim ,with his rifle, each slung over his shoulder, started back over the same ground they'd just come from. According to Willie's calculations they would need forty-two minutes to get into position. Fortunately, Harry and Jim both carried pocket watches so they would know when the other group was ready.

Harry was chomping at the bit to go after the men on the other side of the hill "I came here to fight, Ty. All I want is two minutes with those guys, that's all, and we'll know where they're holding the girl."

Tyler put a hand on the big man's shoulder. "Easy there, big fella. You'll get your chance." He glanced down at the watch. "In about thirty-seven minutes."

With ten minutes to go, the two men once again were at the top of the hill. The two kidnappers were still where they'd last seen them. At the two-minute mark, another figure appeared from the rise behind them coming toward them. A distinctly feminine shape appeared, her voice echoing over to the men, who looked up, then quickly rose to stand by the fire.

"Put out the fire," said the woman, as she arrived beside the two men.

Her fiery beauty and lithe figure were truly breathtaking. Harry looked slack jawed at Tyler who shrugged. With his index finger he indicated they were one minute from executing the plan.

As the second hand swept slowly across the white face of the watch Tyler felt a trickle of sweat run down his back. *This might not work as well I'd hoped.*

At the appointed moment Tyler changed plans, but didn't have time to tell the others, he hoped they would follow along. He suddenly stood up from the grass.

"Hey you!" he shouted, running down the hill. The watch and binoculars were left where he had lain, along with a puzzled Harry who had the presence of mind to lay unmoving and as flat as he could on the ground.

The red-haired woman's mouth hung open as her face registered surprise. Both she and the two men froze where they stood, like deer caught in the open. Tyler moved quickly, and was soon ten yards from the trio. He reached behind his back where he'd secreted the Peacemaker. He'd pulled it out and cocked the hammer before the three kidnappers could reach for their weapons.

Just then Tyler heard the report of a rifle and a shotgun going off over the rise ahead. Willie and Jim had started at the appointed time.

"Hold it. Now drop your gun belts." Tyler said, his voice hard and his eyes fixed in a determined gaze. The two men hesitated, they each stole a glance at the woman, who nodded. *Damn, she's the leader.*

The men undid their belts, their revolvers still in their holsters, and they fell heavily to the ground at their feet.

The beautiful, red-haired woman appeared to be unarmed. Though from the way she carried herself, she probably carried a deadly sting somewhere on her person. She glared at him with hatred in her eyes.

"Kick your holsters toward me." Tyler continued to watch the men, making sure that they did nothing threatening.

The men did as he instructed. There was a burst of gun fire over the hill, Tyler wondered if Willie and Jim were okay.

Fire in their Hearts

According to the plan they were to only cause a distraction, not get into a pitched gun battle with these outlaws.

"You're outnumbered, mister," the woman said with an arrogant sneer that twisted her features. Tyler thought she had been a beautiful woman, but not now.

"I agree, Miss…?"

She grimaced. "You don't need to know who I am. You and your pals will be dead soon, and the little princess will be, too, unless I get what I came for."

Tyler shifted to his right, his eyes focused on the trio. He moved cautiously toward the horses and kept the pistol aimed at the woman. The two men wouldn't be much of a threat as long as he kept the pistol pointed at her. She was important, that much was clear.

"I want to know who's behind this operation." Tyler stepped up beside the first horse. While keeping his eyes trained on the outlaws he managed to undo the reins holding the animal to the rotted log. The reins dropped into the dust.

The woman laughed her eyes hard. She shook her head. "Sorry, mister, you don't need to know."

Tyler cast her a half smile, one side of his mouth turned upward. "Really? Well, I think me and my Peacemaker here don't agree with you." He tipped the barrel of the six-gun to emphasize his point toward her. " I do need to know."

Crossing her arms under the swell of her breasts she sneered at him. The woman's arrogance surprised him. "You wouldn't shoot me. You hero-types are just too *moral*. Besides, you need me if you're going to get to my boss."

So there is someone else behind this plot.

130

"Listen, lady, I'm being paid by Mr. Philip Walker to retrieve the girl and if that means shooting you, then that's what I'll do. It's Walker's problem who's behind the kidnapping, not mine."

Doubt flashed across the woman's features at the mention of Walker's name. Her lips parted to speak when another figure appeared from over the hill behind them, clutching his chest.

A man, someone he didn't know, stumbled forward, dropped to his knees, then fell face first onto the ground. He rolled like a sack of potatoes down the hill until the body came to rest between the outlaws and Tyler. He could see by the way the man's legs and arms flopped as he rolled that he was dead. The neat black hole in the middle of the man's forehead confirmed Tyler's suspicions as the corpse came to rest on its back close to them.

There was a shout as the forth man appeared. He ran over the hill toward them holding a Winchester. His stubble-covered face was decidedly pale for a man used to being outdoors. "They're right behind me!" he shouted to the group below him.

He came to a sudden halt when he saw Tyler. He started lifting his rifle to his shoulder and aimed the long barrel at Tyler. Tyler knew he'd need to move in the next second if he wanted to live, but before he had a chance to react, there was an echo of a rifle report.

Then the rifle slipped from the fourth man's grasp to fall at his feet. His features showed surprise. Tyler saw a growing circle of red in the center of his gray work shirt. The man looked down at the red spot, then his eyes rolled up as he dropped to his knees. An eerie moan escaped his lips before he fell forward to lie still. Tyler could smell blood on the wind.

The woman and her remaining companions seized this opportunity and disappeared into the tall grasses along with their gun belts. Tyler felt a shiver run down his spine like someone had just walked over his grave.

Not good. That was too close.

A mass of short dark red hair popped up from the tall grass to his left. Harry, of course. "I got the bastard," said the big Scot, his face spilt by a wide grin. He looked like some happy kid on his birthday as he stomped down the grassy knoll hurrying toward Tyler.

Tyler frowned. He hadn't wanted to kill the outlaws unless they'd had no other choice. Considering he'd been about to be shot dead by the corpse now lying face-down in the dirt, he knew that Harry had done the right thing. Harry certainly hadn't shot the other one who came over the hill, so Willie or young Jim was responsible for that. Tyler shrugged, somehow he doubted it was Jim.

The question now was where was Victoria, and where had the woman and her companions disappeared to?

He glanced at the one horse he'd managed to untie and realized it hadn't moved even with the shots being fired. The beginning of an idea crept into his mind. Harry came up to him and immediately noticed the thoughtful expression on his face. "Oh, oh, you have another plan, don't you?"

"Yup." Tyler nodded. Gazing at the dead bodies of the two cowboys he shook his head and hoped this one would work out better than the last one.

Twelve

VICTORIA LAY ON the hard rock-covered ground, squirming as she pulled hard against the bonds that again held her hands behind her back. At the same time she tried to loosen and spit out the length of dirty cloth they'd used as a gag. The ropes burned her wrists as she struggled.

Each time there was a shot fired, it made her fear the worst. Maybe her rescuers had been murdered by these villains.

It was no use, the ropes were too tight. She lay under a stand of pine trees, the earthy smell of cast-off needles mingled with the brown soil beneath the trees. The crows had been calling loudly to each other earlier from tree branches high overhead but had stopped when the sound of gunfire echoed across the meadows between the rolling hills. Now an alarming quiet had settled over the forest. It seemed as if everything was holding its breath, waiting.

Suddenly a shadow fell over her, interrupting her thoughts of escape. Rose and Armstrong, sweating, breathing hard, their chests heaving, stood there. Rose's long scarlet hair was a tangled mess. As they stood next to Victoria, Armstrong looked about warily, gripping his rifle in red-knuckled hands.

Victoria had heard the gun shots and now there were only two of the kidnappers left.

The odds were improving for her.

She'd have to stay alert and maybe she'd get a chance to escape.

"Untie her feet and hands, we'll bring her with us," said Rose in a hoarse whisper.

Armstrong dropped to one knee as he rested his rifle against a tree and moved to roll Victoria out into the bright sunlight of the meadow. She was forced to close her eyes as his rough hands untied the ropes behind her back. He undid the ropes that bound her legs, drawing them over her booted feet until she could again move her numb limbs. She was really becoming annoyed at the way these people were treating her.

"Leave the gag," Rose said. "Let's go."

Victoria felt a hand grip her right arm with a vice-like pressure as she was led off into the forest. The tree branches scratched her face as she was led through heavy brush.

They finally came to a stop in a glen near a stand of ancient cedar trees. Rivulets of scars ran up the gnarled bark. Mighty branches were heavy and sagged to the ground. The base of the massive trees was covered in large, spiky pinecones, their tips sharp as razors. They looked like small cone-shaped structures built by some mad architect rather than the works of Mother Nature.

Rose glared at Victoria as she pulled her large knife from the sheath on her belt. She held the polished steel blade to Victoria's throat. "Try anything, missy, and I'll be pleased to cut you a new smile."

Victoria's eyes went wide with fear and she nodded. Rose meant what she said, so for now she'd have to follow the outlaw's instructions. But she also knew that when the window of opportunity presented itself she was going to take it. *"I'll show you, missy."*

Rose stepped back and sheathed her blade. "We need the horses."

Armstrong nodded, his eyes hard as he scanned the trees around them. The trees shielded them, but also provided equal cover for a surprise attack. Armstrong disappeared into the trees. It sounded like he was doubling back to get their horses.

Rose had her back to Victoria, her arms crossed in front of her chest as she watched Armstrong, Her rifle was propped up against a tree.

Victoria inched her way toward the weapon, hoping to get hold of it before Rose saw her. She kept her eyes focused on the back of Rose's head, willing her not to move or look behind her.

Victoria edged along slowly, closer, closer until finally with a small leap she knew she would be able to get her grasp on the gun. In the quiet a twig broke beneath her. The snapping sounded like a gun being fired. Victoria leapt for the rifle. She sprang forward as Rose spun and reached for the knife on her hip. Victoria came up with the rifle pointed at Rose. The rifle wasn't cocked. Victoria watched Rose pull out and throw her knife in one smooth motion. The air next to Victoria was cut with the sound of a knife rushing toward her.

Victoria pulled back the lever as fast as she could, but she felt a stabbing pain as the knife dug high into the left side of her chest.

"That's enough," said a familiar male voice. Victoria looked up through eyes filled with pain at the grinning, handsome image of Tyler Scott. He was leading a horse through the trees as he held a six-gun pointed at Rose.

Victoria felt the rifle slip from her grasp as relief washed over her. Darkness once again crept in from the edges of her vision to engulf her. As she collapsed, her final thought was of Tyler.

Fire in their Hearts

How handsome he looked, his dark curly hair disheveled, his face with that perpetual silly grin. Like a bolt of lightning from a clear blue sky a realization hit her. Since she had met Tyler she hadn't even once thought of Herbert. She was in love with Tyler.

She realized Herbert was someone she had an obligation to, but not even an affection for.

"Why?" she whispered softly as the light began to diffuse into every color of the rainbow. It faded into blackness and began to close around her.

A disembodied voice asked a confusing question, "Who is she talking to?"

The world disappeared, swirling into an inky mass blocking out the sun as a deep coldness invaded her body.

***

Victoria's eyes fluttered open to see a whitewashed canvas ceiling. Wherever she was, she felt cold. Even though she was covered with scratchy woolen blankets, she shivered.

She scanned her surroundings, though her head throbbed every time she moved. There was a small, waist-high table next to the cot she lay on. On the table were some bottles, one brown, one clear, and one green. There were bandages, a variety of knives and other surgical tools. She was in a hospital, though it looked every bit as primitive as the ones she'd seen in some grisly pictures her fiancé had shared with her of the wounded during the American Civil War over twenty years ago.

Heavy blankets were tucked up to her chin. Although it was summer and they looked warm, she felt cold. *How long have I lain here*? She didn't have any recollection.

There was a little light visible against the white canvas side of the tent wall next to her.

With one trembling hand she touched the canvas. It felt warm. Her hand flopped down on top of the scratchy blanket. She heard voices murmuring in the distance, getting louder as they came closer. She wanted to get up and run, but her body refused to cooperate. She tried to lift her head, but the room began to spin so she let it sink back to the pillow. Spots of color danced before her eyes.

Two shadowy figures entered the tent through the front flap. From a great distance she heard a voice call her name. It was a deep male voice, with an edge of concern in it she'd not heard in a long time.

The world disappeared again as her heavy eyelids closed, shutting out the shapes and voices around her.

***

"What do you think, doc?" Tyler rose from the stool where he sat next to Victoria's cot. Looking down at Victoria he saw her chest rise and fell in a gentle rhythm.

Doctor Smithers, a man in his mid-forties, balding with a fringe of brown hair tinged with gray, looked at Tyler then down at Victoria. The doctor's shirt sleeves were tightly rolled up his arms. He peered at the young woman's face, his brow knitted with concern. He reached out with one hand, gently lifted her hand and with his other hand held her left wrist as he felt for the rhythm of her pulse.

"Since my office was destroyed, I know the accommodation in this tent isn't ideal, but we're doing everything we can."

The doctor shook his head, as his watery turquoise eyes moved upward to gaze at Tyler. "It's too early to tell. She's lost a lot of blood and the blow to her head when she fell against that tree may have caused a severe concussion. This is the first sign we've had in four days of a recovery.

What we need to do is to try to wake her up again."

Tyler strode forward he and lifted Victoria's limp body from the cot.

The red-haired woman had escaped into the woods with her male partner when Tyler had appeared in the clearing. Tyler had rushed to grab Victoria. The kidnappers had seen their opportunity to escape and had taken it. The horses had followed their owners into the woods. Tyler remember the fear that filled his gut as he sat on the hard ground, cradling Victoria in his arms and yelling for his own companions.

Tyler had carried Victoria back to town while Harry, Jim, and Willie stayed behind and continued the search for the kidnappers. They hadn't returned from their search yet. It would be dark soon, the last of the golden rays of the sun were dipping below the surface of the ocean out to the west.

Tyler gently raised Victoria's limp body to a sitting position, and tentatively tapped her right cheek. "Victoria. Victoria, wake up," he whispered. He then drew her tightly to him to try and add his warmth, strength, and heartbeat to hers. She murmured softly in his ear and he felt her warm breath against his neck.

He pushed away the thoughts that leapt to mind. Now was not the time. The problem was that he was falling in love with this woman, and sensed that she was beginning to have feelings for him, too. Her fire and spirit had attracted him the moment he met her. She was something special. Something worth fighting for. Victoria was a unique woman with secrets that someone wanted very badly. Whoever was behind these events was desperate enough to kill her to get them. She needed his help, and he wanted to help her.

She stirred, her grip on his shoulder tightening as she nuzzled into his shoulder.

He held her gently as a newborn babe in his strong arms. Rocking her, he began to softly hum an old lullaby he'd heard a long time ago.

He eased Victoria back. Studying her porcelain features, he reached out and, stroking her cheek, watched as her light blue eyes fluttered lazily open to gaze at him. It was as if she were drunk—the doctor had told him it would seem that way, at least at first.

"Water?" Victoria asked softly. Tyler looked at the doctor.

"Only a little," the doctor instructed as he checked Victoria's pulse again. He handed Tyler a tin cup filled with cool water from the well outside

"Where am I?" she said in a hoarse whisper. Her throat was dry.

Tyler lifted the cup to her lips and she took one small sip. She coughed as the water slid down her parched throat. A frown crossed her smooth forehead then she relaxed. She took another deeper sip of water before Tyler set the cup on the small wooden table next to the cot.

"You're safe," he said, softly running one hand over her blonde hair to reassure her. He smiled at her as her blue eyes gazed into his.

"Thank you," she murmured and closed her eyes with a small smile on her lips and curled into his arm to cuddle against him.

He gently lay her down as she began to take deep, even breaths.

"I've never seen anything like it. It's a bloody miracle," said the doctor, who'd been standing off to the side watching them.

"Call it what you will, Doc. She's the strongest, most determined woman I've ever met. She has a real fire in her heart."

Tyler stood and gazed down at her, his own jaw clenching with determination.

"I'll be back," he said. "If there's any change send someone to get me at the Brighton Hotel."

The doctor nodded as Tyler swept past him and out of the medical tent.

Once outside he met Harry. The big man's face was filled with annoyance and was redder than ever.

"Any luck?" Tyler asked looking up at the tall man.

The big Irish blacksmith shook his massive head. Tyler nodded, disappointed even though it was the answer he'd expected. These outlaws were good, very good, and it would take all his skill to stop them. Unfortunately surprise would not be on their side the next time they meet.

"Stay here and guard Victoria," said Tyler. "I'll be at the hotel."

Harry nodded as he crossed his massive arms across his chest and sat in an unpainted wooden chair near the entrance to the medical tent. The chair looked small with the large man's bulk sitting on it. His look of grim determination would signal anyone who tried to enter the tent they'd better not cross him.

Tyler smiled to himself then turned and walked away knowing Victoria would be safe as long as Harry's body held a single breath. He also knew the man had a revolver stuffed inside his shirt as a backup to punctuate his point, if needed.

He'd ask Willie to relieve Harry when he returned from searching the woods close to town. He knew he couldn't stray far from town because the outlaws could be waiting behind the next tree to ambush him and his companions.

***

Several days later there still hadn't been any sign of the outlaws, but Victoria had healed enough that she was allowed to go back to the hotel.

Tyler was pleased that Victoria was not strong enough to go out to the Walkers, he wanted her in town so he could protect her. The Walkers were still an unknown to him and hadn't earned his trust yet. They had let Victoria get kidnapped once and until he found out who was behind that and why he wanted to keep her close.

It was far better to let the outlaws come out into the daylight so he could see them, but Tyler knew instinctively that they'd come at night. At least that's what he'd do in their position.

As he walked, he glanced at the sky and saw the color had shifted to golden orange as the sun began to disappear from the sky. It would disappear into the Pacific Ocean, signaling an end to another day. Jim and Willie had decided to try to track the kidnappers, but said they would come into town to meet up after a couple of days if they hadn't found anything. They would no doubt be back by morning. Right now he had some business to discuss with a certain hotel owner.

By the time Tyler reached the hotel steps the first cool white stars of evening had begun to appear in the deep purple sky. The breeze was cooler now and a slight chill ran through him. He shivered involuntarily.

He started up the wooden steps. The gas lights were lit inside the hotel, giving it a warm glow. Mrs. Smart stood behind the front desk, writing something in a black notebook, her eyes focused on the book.

Tyler opened the door, and the bell over the door frame tinkled brightly announcing his arrival. Mrs. Smart glanced up to see who was coming in.

Her eyes registered surprise upon seeing him, then the look changed to a worried expression. Her hand holding the quill trembled slightly as her eyes shifted to the door behind her. With her fingers poised above the notebook, she froze in place like some ancient Greek statue carved from the finest marble.

Interesting, I should keep an eyes on her.

She wore a frost green-and-white dress, and her hair was in its usual bun, pulled tightly above her pale face.

Tyler had kept himself busy visiting Victoria in the medical tent and playing at the different card games in town. People were starting to drift into Vancouver and were brushing up on their skills before the big game.

He looked at Mrs. Smart and nodded.

"Mr. Scott, I'm so glad to see you're all right." She gave him a thin smile, her sincerity unconvincing.

"Yes, I'm sure you are. Where's Hank? I need to talk to him."

"Huh…I'm not sure. He might be in the saloon. Since Willie ran off he's had to fill in," her voice trailed off.

"Willie didn't run off. He helped me track down Victoria and save her from those murderous cutthroats." Tyler eyes flashed and he felt Mrs. Smart's resolve weakening.

Mrs. Smart's eyes wavered and filled with fear. "You'd better talk to Hank about that."

"You know more than you're telling me, Mrs. Smart, much more. I get the feeling that between you, Hank, the Walkers, and Victoria I'm only getting little bits of the picture," Tyler said, interrupting the visibly frightened woman.

"No. She doesn't," said a calm, deep, male voice coming from over his right shoulder, a voice he recognized immediately.

Tyler looked behind him and saw Hank Smart standing beside Mayor Diller and Chief Constable McNalley. Their hands were at their sides so Tyler didn't feel threatened, which was some relief at least. He moved his hand down to his waist band and reassured himself that the colt revolver was still there, just in case things did turned ugly.

He closed his coat with one hand then turned to face the three men. "Perhaps we'd better talk," said Tyler slowly, a deep frown wrinkling his forehead.

Hank sighed as he glanced at Mayor Diller who nodded, then dropped his eyes in an act of remorse. It was like he was unable to look Tyler in the eyes. McNalley still looked stoic in his navy blue jacket with its makeshift brass buttons that ran down over his ample stomach. His handlebar mustache was freshly waxed, its tips curling upward to form two sweeping loops. His dark, beady eyes were hard as granite as he studied Tyler.

Tyler concluded the rough star of office stitched over his left breast was likely tarnished beyond repair. Perhaps now he'd get the answers that would explain what this was all about.

"Let's go to the saloon," said Hank, breaking the silence.

Tyler nodded and the four men headed for the dinning room and entrance to the saloon. A white-faced Emily Smart watched the men leave, her hands still trembling with fear.

"God help them," she breathed as she watched them go.

Tyler heard her whispered words before the door closed behind him.

Thirteen

TYLER, DILLER, AND McNALLEY took seats in the empty saloon on four rough-hewn oak chairs surrounding a round pine table. Hank went to the bar. He returned with a whiskey bottle and four glasses on a serving tray. He poured them each a shot and set the bottle on the table.

The chief constable had pulled his own mug of beer from the tap behind the bar before he took his seat. He sat, sipping the beer, his dark eyes angry, calling for murder over the rim of the foam-topped glass.

Tyler noted the 'closed' sign hung over the door that led to the street, and the heavy, floor-length curtains covering the windows.

The curtains were the color of blood that had dried in the noonday sun. Hank lit a gas lamp. The flame made the room glow with a warmth that wasn't present among the four men now seated at the table. The air was musty, thick as the mood that permeated the barroom.

"What's with the curtains?" asked Tyler with a half-smile on his lips.

"Ladies don't like us being in here drinking," said Hank.

Tyler knew of the women's movement to keep men out of the saloons. Their goal was to make Vancouver a decent city in which to raise their children. The city had a rough frontier reputation from the blue collar workforce that drove the local economy. The lumberjacks, mill workers, dock hands, miners, and fishermen worked hard, and they liked to play hard, too.

Tyler nodded then took a sip of the whiskey. It burned as it traveled down his throat. It wasn't the best he'd ever tasted, but not the worst either. The taste and odor was different from the Tennessee whiskey he'd had in San Francisco. *But then I'm not in California any more, am I?* Of course, if this went badly it was very likely he'd wouldn't be breathing the nice clean air in Canada or anywhere else for that matter.

"Prefer corn whiskey myself," he said casually, feeling three pairs of eyes staring at him.

"It's made from rye," said Diller, his voice deep, his eyes steady and serious. Until now Tyler had considered the man a fool, but the eyes contained a determination that had finally revealed itself. *Perfect for a politician.*

Tyler nodded and took another sip, slowly savoring it. "Well, it's different."

"Screw the whiskey," said McNalley, his voice betraying his impatience, "we got other things to discuss."

Diller leaned forward, his elbows resting on the arms of his chair. "The chief constable is correct, Mr. Scott. We need your help."

Before he could stop himself Tyler's eyebrows arched upward registering his surprise. He'd expected to be threatened or at a minimum run out of town. *They needed my help? Something really isn't right about all this.*

145

Hank for his part looked nervous, he was busy fidgeting with his hands underneath the table while McNalley looked clearly annoyed. Somehow Tyler didn't think his being asked to help was the consensus of opinion around the table.

"What do you want from me?" Tyler asked after placing his glass on the table and easing back in his chair. His long fingers were intertwined in his lap, ready, if need be, to reach for his gun.

Diller shrugged then continued. "You appear to be a resourceful man, a natural leader." Tyler nodded with a smirk, his dark eyes focused on the mayor's cherubic features.

McNalley lifted his glass to his lips and glared at the gambler, his cheeks growing a little redder. *At this rate, those red chipmunk cheeks might even start to match his nose.*

"Gentlemen, I'm merely a small-time gambler passing through on my way back east. What possible assistance could I offer you?"

Diller smiled in the way politicians liked to do. "Mr. Scott, we want you to call off the search for the kidnappers, and help us get Miss Kelly out of Vancouver and on her way home."

Tyler shook his head and righted his chair. "And why should I do that?"

"Because you'll be well paid, that's why. There'll be enough compensation that you'll have a very healthy stake for the poker gathering."

A pay off? These bastards were willing to pay him off, which meant he'd become an annoyance to whoever was behind all this. If they wanted Victoria out of town maybe it was her that they were worried about? *But who was the mastermind?*

Like the good poker player he was, he needed time to draw them out and reveal their hole card.

146

"How much are we talking about? Exactly." He paused, leaned back in his chair again and waited for them to answer his question.

Diller glanced at his co-conspirators and leaned forward as if someone would overhear what he was about to reveal. "Five thousand."

Now Tyler was truly shocked. He held his face in a tight grin as he considered his next move. That was a princely sum! He felt the stakes had suddenly been raised. Time to play his trump card and suffer the consequences later.

"When will I get paid?"

"As soon as Miss Kelly boards the eastbound train in New Westminster," blurted McNalley, not waiting for Diller to speak up. Diller cast him a withering stare, the big man merely nodded at him with a look of annoyance on his face.

McNalley was certainly no politician and obviously had little patience for negotiation. He was used to getting his own way around town as the only *real copper*. Tyler made a note of this personality flaw. He was sure it would come in handy later.

"Who's paying the bill? From what I've seen around here, there isn't a lot of money to go around." The amused edge was gone from Tyler's voice, his eyes narrowed as his lips pressed together in a thin red line.

Diller shook his head. "Sorry, that's information you don't need. All you have to know is if the money is available, if you cooperate. It is." He paused. "What I can tell you is you'll have the stake you need to set yourself up very nicely back east. I hear there's a lotta dollars in the card rooms in Montreal and Toronto." Diller shrugged and he meet Tyler's gaze. "We might even manage a few key introductions to get you into the high stakes games."

Now Tyler's interest was piqued. These blackguards were playing on the knowledge of his purpose for being here in the first place. But how did they learn he was desperate to get to the east and make some real cash? *Have I said anything to anyone or were they just guessing?*

"Who says I need help? I was planning to go back east on my own after the tournament in Vancouver. I fully expect to be well set up to play with the big boys after I win here." Tyler punctuated his words with a wry smile and righted his chair.

Diller glanced at McNalley with a pained expression. They obviously hadn't expected him to side step them so neatly. They thought he was some dumb Yank who could be bought off. *Maybe I'd better back down for now. I don't like the odds at the moment. Three of them, and only one of me.*

Even though he was younger and stronger than each of them individually, three was taking too much of a chance. He'd bide his time and wait for an opening. *Besides, if these three were in cahoots with the kidnappers then they might lay a trap for me and Victoria.* He didn't mind taking chances himself, but he wasn't about to put Victoria in jeopardy. Not after what she'd just been through.

Tyler smiled widely, exposing twin rows of ivory teeth. "Sorry, guys just havin' a little fun." He shrugged. "Sure, I'll take your money to make sure Miss Victoria makes her way to the train station. When do you want her there?"

Diller looked relieved, but the tips of McNalley's ears had become red beacons that could've lit the room even better than the light from the oil lamp. The big man gritted his teeth, raised his glass to his lips, and grunted into it as he took a large swallow of the whiskey. He glared at Tyler as if he was contemplating a small rodent that he was about to squash beneath his boot heel.

"Well, that's more like it, Mr. Scott. We'd like Miss. Victoria on the train Friday morning at nine o'clock. If you leave here on Thursday and overnight it should work out just fine," said Diller cheerily. "Yes, I believe we can come to some financial arrangement,"

Diller nodded at Hank who reached inside the black vest he wore over his white shirt and pulled a wad of bills from within, then placed them on the table. Until now Hank had sat calmly watching the proceeding with an almost bemused expression on his face. His fingers intertwined in his lap. His own glass of whiskey sat untouched in front of him, the scent permeating the air.

Tyler decided there was far more to this man than being a simple innkeeper. Tyler eyed the stack of bills tied with a length of rough-hewn twine. That was a lot of money sitting there.

"Consider this a down payment. The rest will be paid at the train station once she boards."

Tyler shrugged and picked up the wad of crumpled bills. He slipped the wad of paper into the pocket of his woolen coat. His normally sensitive fingertips came alive from the touch and rubbing of the roughened threads of the fabric. Anger burned in Tyler's belly, but he kept his face calm. These men were desperate to get Victoria and him out of town as soon as possible. They had to be connected to the kidnapping. When it failed, they were willing to pay big bucks to get rid of their problem? Why didn't they just kill her? None of this made any sense.

If the city elders were involved in this mess, then who else was behind the plot? *I need a lot more information.*

"What time does the next carriage leave for New Westminster?" he said, his voice as casual as he could make it. He pressed back in the chair, now resting on the balls of his feet.

149

He tipped his hat back with one finger to reveal his deep brown eyes that scanned the three men before him. His right hand casually brushed the six-gun that hung off his hip in its brown leather holster.

"Two o'clock," grunted McNalley, who then belched to relief himself of the air he'd just swallowed with the last of the warm beer in his mug.

"Okay," said Tyler. With a reassuring smile he rose from the chair, pushing backward causing it to scrape across the wood planks of the floor.

"And don't be late, Scott. If you know what I mean."

Tyler knew by the look the chief constable gave him the big man would enjoy teaching him a lesson if he were late. Guys like McNalley got their kicks by hurting others. He'd seen it before. It usually meant he'd worn out his welcome and it was time to move on, so he promptly left the town or city he was in. This time it was different. This time someone had offered him money to leave, somehow it felt wrong. They'd also threatened a beautiful young woman's life.

Tyler wasn't leaving until he found out who was responsible and why.

Fourteen

TYLER ARRIVED BACK at the hotel to find Willie watching the lobby, making sure that no unwelcome guests came to call on Miss Victoria. His shotgun rested across his muscular arm. He cradled as if it were a newborn infant. A grim smile was fixed on his dusky features. His dark eyes danced with impatience as he stood in a relaxed posture that could become instantly lethal should the need arise.

"Hey, Ty," the bartender said, as Tyler came into the lobby. The smell of dust met Tyler's nostrils as he closed the door behind him. "Willie, how did it go?" he acknowledged the man with a tight grin.

"We followed their tracks for a while, but lost them in the valley. We tried to pick them up on the other side, but couldn't find anything with all the rock and shale." Willie shook his head, his lips pinched together in a tight line.

"Where's Victoria?"

Willie nodded toward the staircase that led to the upper floors. "She's in her room."

"Mr. Scott, I have a letter for Miss Victoria I was just going to take up to her," Mrs. Smart said as she held a white envelope in her hand.

Fire in their Hearts

"I'll take it up for you and give it to her if you like." Tyler looked at Mrs. Smart and walked over to her.

"Why thank you, that's much appreciated."

Tyler turned and walked to the stairs. He took the steps two at a time until he was on the second floor, he turned down the hall and was soon standing outside Victoria's door. He knocked gently. "Victoria. It's Tyler Scott."

"Just a moment," came her soft voice through the thick wooden door.

After several seconds the door opened, and Tyler gasped. Victoria wore a soft, billowing blue hat, her long flowing blonde curls spilled over her bare, milky white shoulders. She wore a thin paisley dress that covered her and a smile that would have brightened the gloomiest night. Her azure eyes danced with delight as she saw him. The sweet perfume she wore wafted over him, completing the seduction. She stepped back to admit him and slammed the door behind them.

Throwing her arms around his neck, she pulled his body close to hers. He could feel the warm curves of her body underneath her dress as his strong hands slipped down to her waist. Her full, hungry lips pressed into his. Their eyes opened and they gazed into each others' souls, two hearts on fire, with a powerful desire neither of them had ever experienced before. He felt her soft wet tongue slip between his lips. His tongue played with hers, a duel of desire. His hands roamed her body.

Her ripe body felt lush in his hands. Her wide hips and full breasts were soft beneath his touch. Desire burned deep from within. They separated and she grasped his hand in hers as they shyly went to the metal-framed bed across the room.

152

"How are you feeling, Victoria?" Tyler asked as he looked into her eyes with concern.

"Still a little weak sometimes, but I'm getting stronger every day. I'm looking forward to the challenge."

Tyler led her to the bed. He sat down; looking up at her he smiled . She sat down at the head of the bed and leaned into the soft pillows.

He smiled at her, got up and went to the other side of the bed so she could stretch out. She made herself comfortable. When she was settled, he carefully lay down beside her and she rolled over to lay her head on his chest. He held her very gently in his arms, mindful of her injuries, her breathing was soft against his face.

"Tyler?" Victoria shifted.

"Yes…my love." Tyler realized with a start that he was in love, and had been since he'd first laid eyes on Victoria. He stiffened and held completely still, he didn't want to scare her, she had been through so much in the past few days.

He felt Victoria hold her breath.

"Is there something wrong?" Tyler asked.

"No. It's just that I've never been in love before, not really," she said in a soft voice, barely above a whisper.

He felt her nod against his chest, her fingers stroking his chest as he continued. "I thought I was once, but I was wrong. Until this moment I've never really cared for or felt for anyone the way I do you."

"Oh Ty, how can we—" She lifted her head to look into his eyes. She stopped speaking as she pressed one long finger against his lips. "Can we talk about this later? Right now I want to enjoy the moment."

He nodded and fell silent, holding her in his arms. His mind whirled with confusion. He loved her, his knees went weak at the sight of her, he knew he would sacrifice himself to protect her. He was not accustomed to losing control of any situation. Somehow Victoria had made him do things he didn't normally do. *I must be in love. It's the only possible explanation.*

As they held each other, Tyler could feel Victoria's heart beat slow as his strong arm relaxed around her. He stroked her hair as he closed his eyes. He smiled as she snuggled close to him, she was safe and protected now. He'd make sure that she stayed that way, then he let himself relax too.

***

In another of the surviving hotels, The Alabaster, Rose Patterson sat on a hard wooden chair sipping from a short glass of whiskey. Across from her sat a young man in a dark woolen uniform.

"I want more," said the young man.

Rose smirked as she placed her glass of the oak-scented liquor on the table that separated them. "What for?"

"I helped you back in the woods. They wanted to capture one of the men and I killed him for you. He might've talked."

One of Rose's dark red eyebrows arched on her pale forehead. "True, but then again you might also talk."

The young blond man's face paled, fear appeared in the corner of his pale blue eyes. "Now why would I do that?"

"Because sooner or later that Scott feller is gonna figure out it was you who killed my man. When he does, you're gonna talk."

The man trembled and his right hand dropped to his side beneath the table. He slid his six-gun out from under his coat and was about to cock the hammer when a deafening shot rang out in the room. The air was filed with the odor of burnt gun powder.

154

Young James Nelson would speak no more. The shock registered on his face. His eyes clouded over, his six-gun slipping from his grasp to fall with a thud on the wooden floor boards. He pitched forward, his head hitting the table hard as pools of blood formed beneath the chair.

"A real shame," said Rose with mock sincerity," such a good-looking kid." She holstered her gun as she glanced over her left shoulder to the man who stood by the window. "Maybe you could say a prayer for him?"

"Immoral men such as he cannot be saved by prayer," said Parson Sloan, his red-rimmed eyes dark slits, his sallow skin tight across his narrow face. He looked like a lean wolf about to pounce on its prey.

Rose smirked. "Yeah. I know what you mean."

She picked up her shot of whiskey and drained the glass. She stood, crossing to the door, pulling it open, she stuck her head out into the hall. Miles Armstrong sat in a wooden chair with spokes pressing against his back, his hat pulled down over his eyes, the chair leaning back against the wall.

Rose's features darkened. She was amazed—he had slept through the sound of a gun going off almost next to him. "I don't pay you to snooze, Miles."

Miles leaned forward and the two front legs of the chair hit the bare wood floor with a thud. He pulled the hat brim off his eyes and perched his Stetson atop his nest of brown dirty curls. The dark stubble covering his chin seemed to be getting visibly darker with each passing hour. "No, ma'm," he said, his eyes now open and alert.

Rose thought her hired help smelled more like his horse than a man, which wasn't far from the truth.

Fire in their Hearts

Like most cow-hands she'd met since leaving her father's farm in Texas fifteen years previous, he probably only bathed once a month, if that. At least this time she had the upper hand over the men she met and worked with. Money made her powerful, she liked the feeling it gave her. Men were rats, villains. Her drunken father had raped her when she was twelve and her mother had done nothing to stop him. Once she finished this job she would have the money to stay on top for the rest of her life. She would call the shots. No man would ever tell her what to do or take advantage of her again.

"Get in here and clean up this mess." Her voice was cold.

She left the door open as Miles got up and came inside to find young Jim Nelson slumped over the table. The blood pooling beneath him was already growing cool. Miles moved to stand over the young man's corpse.

"Serves him right for killin' 'ol Pete," he said as he locked his hands underneath Jim's arms and lifted him to an upright position. Jim's eyes were still open, his face a mask of surprise. His head lolled to one side, his mouth hung open as he sat there, lifeless.

Miles reached down and undid Jim's gun belt, lifted it clear of the blood, and placed it on the table. Next he bent down, retrieving the six-gun that had fallen to the floor. It was covered in Jim's blood. Miles lay it on the table next to the gun belt. Rose retrieved one of the towels the innkeeper gave them, and tossed it to Miles.

He wiped down the weapon until the burnished metal of the gun gleamed once again. He wiped the blood off the table, then holstered the gun.

Next he rifled Jim's pockets and found only a few coins totaling two dollars and five cents. "Must've needed the money."

"Don't we all," Rose said evenly.

156

Reaching deep in the dead man's right pocket he found a piece of paper folded into a neat square. He opened the paper and saw there was some writing on it.

"I can't read," he said in a mater-of-fact way.

Rose nodded and snatched the paper from him.

"It says Brighton Hotel, Smart." Her eyes flashed as she tossed the paper on the table. "That must be where they're staying."

Parson Sloan's features broke into a maniacal grin. "We'll need a plan."

Rose nodded a wry smile on her face. Miles shrugged and heaved Jim's corpse up and dragged the dead man from the room, leaving a trail of dark crimson streaks behind him.

***

Tyler woke to find he was in Victoria's bedroom, she was sitting at the table, her robe covering her shoulders. Her intense blue eyes were focused on him.

She frowned as he opened his eyes.

It was the most beautiful frown he'd ever seen on any woman. "Hello, darling," he said as he rolled on his side and propped his head in his right hand. He patted the empty covers beside him with his left. "Why don't you join me?"

Victoria's eyes suddenly brimmed with tears as her face was transformed to an expression of anguish. "I'm sorry, Ty…" her next words caught in her throat.

"What is it? Did I do something wrong?" Tyler slipped out from under the covers. He moved to stand behind her, offering his strong arms to gently comfort her. She stood and was enveloped by him. He pulled her to him, molding her body to his. It was as if they were locked together forever as one body. If only this could be true.

Fire in their Hearts

Salty tears ran down Victoria's cheeks as she trembled in his arms. She buried her head in his chest to muffle her pain and he stroked her hair, trying to comfort her.

He cupped her head and stroked her blond hair. "There, there, my love."

She broke from him, her tear swollen eyes flared with anger. "Don't say that, Ty. You must never say that again."

"I don't understand."

"It's complicated, that's all. I can't see you again. You're going to have to leave me alone."

Tyler couldn't believe what he was hearing. Victoria's words didn't make any sense at all. But if that was her wish and it seemed to be, he would honor it. Nodding slowly he lowered his eyes and moved away from her. Swirling clouds of emotion followed him as he moved to the bed where he sat and pulled on his boots. In a daze he finished buttoning his shirt. He slipped his jacket over his broad shoulders as he turned and stole from the room without saying another word.

***

Victoria dropped onto a nearby chair, her legs trembling. Hot tears streamed down her flushed cheeks. Her body began to tremble uncontrollably as she watched the man she loved leave her. He closed the door gently behind him. Even though she was hopelessly and completely in love with him, she knew this might be the last time she would ever see him.

She'd never felt this way about a man before and knew she never would again. Certainly not her fiancé. But for her family, her father, she had given her word she would marry Herbert and she would do her duty.

Herbert was a hopeless gambler and a drunk. True, his family had money and influence, but she didn't love him. She would never love him, she knew that now. Not like she loved Tyler Scott. She also knew Tyler loved her and that hurt more than she could bear.

Standing, she moved to the bed and threw herself across it as a torrent of tears mushroomed in the loneliness of her room. Once she got her crying in check she remembered her father had sent her a letter. She opened it and was surprised to learn the Crown had named Donald A. Smith and Richard B. Angus as trustees of the Canadian Pacific Railroad lands covering 480 acres in the area of Granville.

Victoria was sure Philip Walker would have been one of the trustees and wondered if the Walkers knew yet and how they were going to react. She also noticed that the area of Granville was mentioned. She remembered that area from the major real estate owners documents and the notation with Mr. Sloan's name next to it.

***

Tyler stood outside Victoria's room in the empty hallway, his mind whirling with confusion. *I'll never understand women.*

His heart ached and his soul burned for her. She was what he'd been looking for all his life and now he'd lost her.

His thoughts were interrupted by Harry, who came storming down the hallway toward him. Harry's pale skin flushed with anger, his bushy red eyebrows knitted into a V on his forehead.

"Ty. I'm glad I found you. Jim's been killed." Harry stood in front of Tyler, the big man's eyes burned with undisguised rage.

Tyler stared at the big blacksmith, dumbfounded. The young, fresh-faced constable dead? *How?* His mind was in turmoil with raw emotions, first sorrow over Victoria, now replaced with anger over the death of Jim. Tyler's jaw tightened. "Who did it?"

"We don't know. His body was found lying in a ditch down the street from the Alabaster 'bout half'n hour ago. He's been shot."

Tyler wondered how a society that abhorred guns could have so many people shooting at each other.

The chief constable. I need to find McNalley. Maybe the fat, useless oaf would finally do something to clean up this mess. Kidnapping. Being shot at by a gang of cutthroats. Bribery. And now murder? What did the stupid son-of-a-bitch need, an invitation to do his job?

"Where's McNalley?" Tyler said, his voice terse, hiding all emotion.

Harry shook his head. "No one's seen him."

Tyler felt the heat rise in his face. "Let's find him."

Harry nodded. "I told Willie, he's in the lobby with his little *buddy.*" Meaning the bartender was ready with his trusty shotgun, if the gang of kidnappers showed themselves. "He'll keep an eye on Victoria while we're gone."

He hoped Hank didn't notice them leave. There was, after all, still the reward money offered by Philip Walker for her safe return to consider. He chastised himself at the thought of the money. Victoria was worth far more to him than money.

Now all they had to do was find the kidnappers before they struck in again, get Victoria safely on the train to the east, and find out who was behind the conspiracy and why? Mind you if they found out who was behind the conspiracy maybe Victoria wouldn't need to leave Vancouver. Maybe they could go back east together.

Tyler rolled his eyes and looked up. *Is that all?* Oh, and not to mention the poker gather he had to win. Tyler sighed as he nodded to Harry. The two men started down the hallway toward the stairs. Tyler thumbed the six-gun in his holster.

It all sounded so easy when you thought about it, but he had a strong feeling that the worst was yet to come.

Fifteen

ROSE PATTERSON, MILES Armstrong, and Parson Sloan walked toward the Brighton Hotel after dumping Jim's body in the ditch. They'd rolled the young man's corpse in a blanket before they left the hotel and they carried him between them. Limp bodies were surprising awkward to carry any distance. Fortunately the drainage ditch wasn't too far from the hotel. Sloan and Miles carried the young constable's body, with Rose acting as director.

They'd waited until just before dawn and no one had seen them with the body. Rose kept a look out for any curious early morning passersby.

As they walked back from dumping the body some of the early risers were already moving about. Mrs. Wallace was headed to her chicken coop to retrieve the morning eggs. She waved at them as they passed. Sloan smiled thinly and tipped his black hat in her direction.

Rose ignored the woman, her mind was focused on the task ahead. Out of the corner of one eye she saw Miles toss Mrs. Wallace one of his patented, lopsided grins. She rolled her eyes in distaste. The guy was a sloppy bastard.

I need to take care of him when this is over.

Now they needed to find Victoria Ann McNichol and get her back in their not-so-soft-and-tender care. The boss wanted her kept under wraps until a decision was made. The railroad was going no farther than New Westminster no matter what Hiram McNichol wanted. The old man's days of power in Canada were about to end. Rose's job was to ensure that his plans for expansion didn't succeed, or she would die trying.

The trio entered the lobby of the Brighton Hotel to find a large black man sitting in a leather wingback chair cradling a shotgun in his lap. He eyed them suspiciously as they entered. His eyes narrowed and a look of recognition crossed his dark features when he saw the parson. He stood, the polished steel barrel of the shotgun pointed downward hung at his side, his finger resting outside the trigger guard ready in case he needed to use the weapon. At this close proximity Rose somehow doubted he'd mange to lift and cock the twin hammers in time to use the gun before they disarmed him or killed him.

Rose glanced at Miles who caught the look in her eyes. He nodded almost imperceptivity. His hard eyes focused on the black man as the parson spoke.

"Hello, Willie." Sloan attempted a friendly grin. His lips were too cruelly thin to reflect anything but a nightmarish sneer. The man's thin face always gave him the appearance more of an undertaker than a man of God. His dark suits, white shirts, and round Quaker hat added to the unfortunate appearance of an undertaker— or least someone who specialized in maters of the dead.

Willie nodded, his feet set apart ready to react to any threat. His gaze traveled across the three faces then back again. "What can I do for you, Parson?" he said slowly.

"We're looking for Miss Victoria McNichol. Do you happen to know where she might be?"

Willie's eyes flitted toward the staircase leading to the upper floors then back to the trio standing before him. "Well, I—" he didn't finish the sentence.

Rose saw Willie's finger twitch near the trigger guard of the shotgun. As if on cue she and Miles both pulled their six-guns from their holsters and fired simultaneously.

The noise of the two guns going off in the confined space of the lobby was deafening. The glass of the windows facing the street seemed to bend outward from the concussion caused by the movement of air as the bullets traveled the short distance between the gangsters and the bartender. The bullets struck Willie simultaneously in the center of his chest. He'd been attempting to raise the shotgun when he'd been hit.

Red spurts of blood shot from the wounds in his chest as his eyes went wide with surprise. Then his grip loosened, the shotgun sagged as he dropped to his knees. The weapon fell to the floor with a clatter. His eyes stared at a spot behind Sloan as he dropped onto his back. He lay still, his sightless eyes still open, looking at the sky.

Sloan turned to glare at his companions with the still smoking Peacemakers in their hands. The air of the lobby was rife with the smell of burnt gun powder and coppery blood. "Did you really have to kill him? We outnumbered him and could easily have overpowered him."

"Take no prisoners," Rose said, her jaw tight, her gaze hard as she looked at the dead bartender laying at their feet. "He could've made trouble for us later."

She holstered her gun as did Miles, and they paused to listen for any sound coming from overhead as Hank and Emily Smart burst into the lobby from the door behind the oak reception desk. They paled as they saw the scene before them. Three people stood in the lobby with a bloodied body laying on the floor. There was an ever-widening stain surrounding Willie's cooling corpse like a halo of red ink.

"What the hell?" said Hank. There was fear in his voice. Emily's hands trembled as she stepped around the desk and crouched beside Willie. She touched him lightly on the neck then quickly pulled her fingers back as if she'd been burned by a hot stove. She looked at up at Rose. "He's dead," she said.

Rose nodded. Her voice was as hard as granite, "Yup, and he deserved it. Helping that no good gambler was his undoing. He shouldn't have interfered. Anyone who gets in my way is gonna end up just like him."

"We don't want no part of any killing. Hank?" She turned and gazed at her husband with pleading eyes.

"That's right," said Hank. "We were assured no one would get hurt when we agreed to help."

"The boss offered no such guarantees. He knows what I have might have to do to get the job done."

"And who might that be?" said a soft feminine voice from over their heads.

All eyes turned to look upward to see Victoria Ann McNichol dressed in a simple gray skirt and a white linen blouse that was buttoned up to her slender neck.

She stood at the top of the stairs with a Winchester carbine trained on the group below.

Her blue eyes were hard as diamonds and her long blonde hair was done up in ringlets under a gray and white hat that matched her skirt. The pale skin of her face and neck was flushed with inner rage.

Rose fingered her weapon as she stepped forward. She held her left hand up and an evil grin crossed her dark complexion. "Now, Miss McNichol, there's no need for any shooting."

Victoria raised the rifle and sighted down the barrel at Rose, who froze in place. Her right hand was still resting on the butt of her revolver. "One more step and you'll have a new bodily orifice," said Victoria. Using the rifle as a pointer she motioned for Rose to step back. "I'd prefer you drop your gun belt and step back with your hands above your head." Victoria moved down two steps, the rifle still aimed at Rose's chest.

From the corner of her eye Rose saw Miles start to draw his revolver. Victoria must have seen it, too, because she swung the Winchester around and fired one quick shot. The bullet entered Miles' left leg and he collapsed with a scream, his hands gripping his leg as blood immediately covered his fingers.

Rose took the opportunity offered by the distraction to break for the front door. She moved as fast as a mountain lion, and was out the door before Victoria could react.

Victoria managed to get one shot off just as the door closed, but missed the fleeing kidnapper. The bullet hit the edge of the doorframe, shattering it.

Hank and Emily had dropped flat to the floor, their hands covering their heads. It was as if they'd become marble statues of people lying on the polished floor.

Victoria moved down the staircase. She stood over Miles Armstrong who was howling in pain.

She dropped to her haunches and retrieved his revolver from his holster and slipped it into the waistband of her skirt.

"Hank. I've had enough," Emily said. She was standing on shaky legs, her hair, normally in a tight bun atop her head, had come loose, was now hanging in front of her face as if it had been twisted by some violent tornado. She blew at one long strand of hair that hung over her flushed face. "It's time we got the chief constable involved, before anyone else gets hurt. It's time to do the right thing." She glared at her husband, her fists on her hips.

Victoria gazed wide eyed at Hank then Emily. *Poor Hank, he better do what she says if he knows what's good for him.*

They'd been so kind to her after the fire. They took her in when Tyler brought her back to civilization. *They were involved?* Her mind whirled with the impact of what had just been revealed. *Where was Tyler? Is he okay?* Her heart seemed to stop and her eyes narrowed as she realized he may be in serious danger.

Treachery was everywhere.

Hank stood and brushed off his heavy cotton pants with trembling hands. He breathed a heavy sigh. "You're right, Em. Enough is enough."

Victoria lowered the rifle to her side, the steel barrel now pointed at the floor. She had killed someone. She started to shake. The weapon suddenly felt like an anvil, as if it weighted more than she was capable of carrying. Her knees felt weaker than ever in her twenty-six years of living. *Oh God, what have I done?*

She took a deep breath and let it out as she composed herself. She needed to think and act now and needed a clear head.

"Who's behind this?" she asked, her voice barely above a whisper. Her steely gaze fell first on Hank, then Emily. Emily had regained her composure.

167

She crossed her arms across her chest and lifted her chin, her expression was one of annoyance as frowns wrinkled her forehead. She stared at her husband whose face reddened as he visibly suffered under the steady accusatory gaze of the two women.

"Enough is enough. Come on, Mr. Smart."

"I need a drink," Hank croaked.

Emily nodded and uncrossed her arms. "I agree, Mr. Smart," she said.

Hank winced. Obviously she only called him by his family name when he was in the greatest of trouble. Emily motioned for Victoria and Hank to follow her as she started for the door that led to the barroom.

Victoria heaved the rifle across her arms and motioned with her head for Hank to follow his wife. He nodded sheepishly and Victoria managed to herd him along, using the barrel of the rifle to urge him forward. Now maybe she'd get some answers.

***

Victoria sat in the dim bar of the Brighton Hotel listening to Hank Smart as he told her about his and his wife's part in what was evidently a conspiracy involving Victoria's father and the westward expansion of the railroad. Some saw the railroad as a threat and others as an opportunity.

A clear glass sat in front of Victoria with a shot of whiskey in it. She hadn't yet tasted the foul-smelling drink. The smell coming from the drink was musky, like the smell of the oak barrel it had been aged in. She abhorred alcohol in all its forms, but hadn't the heart to refuse the glass when Emily had offered. Husband and wife had both drunk theirs before Hank launched into his tale.

Evidently someone, who in his cable identified himself as Smith—obviously a fake name— had contacted Chief Constable McNalley and Mayor Diller, requesting they urge Victoria to leave Vancouver as quickly as possible by whatever means possible.

Diller and McNalley approached the Smarts to help them, since Victoria was staying in their hotel and the Smarts would have easy access to her. They wanted Emily and Hank to encourage Victoria to leave Vancouver after the fire, for which they would be paid handsomely. The money would help them financially, and give them the extra capital they needed for the hotel.

"Starting a new hotel is expensive," said Hank, his eyes puffy and sad as a hound dog's. "We had no idea you'd be kidnapped. We want no part of such things." His voice cracked and a single tear streamed down his left cheek. He shook his head. "It was my fault." He buried his face in his hands, his body shook as a sob escaped his throat.

Emily reached over to run a hand down her husband's back. "There's been too much death, Miss Victoria. Please believe us when we say we had no idea at all this was gonna happen. We would never have gotten involved if we knew their whole plan. Damn that Diller." She spat the mayor's name as if it were poison.

As Victoria gazed at the Smarts, her heart went out to them. It seemed they had been caught in the middle of a diabolical scheme. She had no doubt they were telling the truth. They were pawns and she had to find the person orchestrating the whole operation.

"Where did the telegram come from? What city?" Victoria asked.

Hank raised his head to look at her. "Boston, I think?" He dropped his face back into his hands and wept. "Poor Willie. It's all my fault. I can't undo what happened."

Victoria winced and looked at Emily. *And they call us the weaker sex.*

Emily shook her head. "Yes. It was from Boston. Mayor Diller showed it to me. Otherwise we wouldn't have agreed to help them. We wanted to make sure the money..." she paused and her cheeks flushed pink. "*I* wanted to make sure they weren't conning us. Diller and McNalley aren't the most reliable of men."

Victoria eyes narrowed. "Of that much I'm in agreement with you," she muttered.

She abruptly pushed back her chair, causing it to scrape loudly in the quiet of the barroom then stood up from the table. "We have to find Tyler and the others." Victoria lifted the gun and cradled it in her arms as she walked toward the door. The solid weight of the weapon felt good in her slender hands.

"What're you gonna do?" asked Emily.

"I think I know who's behind the kidnapping and the conspiracy. And I'm damn mad."

Sixteen

Tyler and Harry found Diller and McNalley on Main Street, supervising the building of the new police station and jail. A crew of local craftsmen was busy erecting one of the outside walls of the jail as they walked up. The foreman was shouting to his work crew as they, in unison, pulled the wall upward.

The smell of the dusty street filled the air, and in the heat sweat streamed down the faces of Diller and McNalley. They were dressed in thick dark cotton work pants with white work shirts open at the collar.

The men were pulling the wall upward using ropes attached to wooden pulleys to give them more leverage. There were two men on each rope, and at the foreman's command, they pulled in unison. The wall of nailed two-by-fours moved upward with each heave until it stood upright.

Three men stood nearby, each with a steel hammer in his grip, waiting to drive a large spike through the bottom boards into the flooring, which had already been constructed.

Fire in their Hearts

The overlapping woods planks had been nailed to massive timbers that made up the foundation of the building. As the pulling crew got the wall to stand in place, men with hammers swung in sharp downward strokes, driving the spikes in with single blows. One, two, three, all about twelve inches apart.

It was if they were a single machine, perfectly choreographed as they executed their roles to rebuild the burnt-out city. The men were in their rolled-up shirt sleeves showing their muscular forearms. These were men used to construction for survival. They were typical of the so called 'frontier spirit,' as the eastern newspapers were so fond of labeling such men during the westward expansion years.

"Mayor, Chief," said Tyler, as he and Harry strode up to the two men who controlled the town.

Diller and McNalley turned and stared at the two men approaching them, a look of astonishment on their faces. "I thought you were leaving town yesterday," said Diller. He cast a worried glance at McNalley who frowned, his face darkened by anger. Tyler had come to learn the chief constable wasn't a man known for his patience. *That will be his undoing.*

Tyler raised one hand to stop the chief constable before he spoke. "The situation has changed. Jim is dead. Murdered."

The chief's expression relaxed to one of astonishment. "What?"

Tyler continued. "His body was found in a ditch down the street from the Alabaster."

McNalley nodded, his features grim, his lips pursed. Tyler could see the conflicting emotions travel across the man's wide face. His beady eyes were hard and reflected his disgust with what had happened to his young constable.

"Did he have a gun with him?"

"We don't know. The body's at Doc O'Hara's office. Maybe he'll have more detailed information for us."

McNalley's eyes narrowed. "What do you mean, *us*?"

Tyler shrugged. "Harry and I liked young Jim, and we want to help you find his killer. If that's okay with you, Chief?"

When the chief hesitated Diller jumped in. "Com'on, Bill, you know you could use the help. And after all, Jim was helping them when he was killed."

McNalley regarded his boss, who nodded his head, as his shoulders slumped in a resignation of defeat.

"Okay, let's go see the doc." McNalley said.

Diller patted McNalley on the back and the four men strode toward the doctor's office.

Doctor Walter O'Hara was originally from Toronto, and had studied medicine at the prestigious McGill University Faculty of Medicine. Why he had moved west was a mystery, one the doctor had never discussed with anyone.

He was a distinguished looking man with traces of grey at the temple. While he had never revealed his age, speculation among the women in town was that the handsome physician, with sparkling hazel eyes, was in his late thirties or early forties. He was unmarried, and had never been known the seek the company of the unattached local women. Not that there was a lot of choice amongst the decent single women of this frontier city.

The men arrived at his office to find him dressed in a white cotton apron that covered his street clothes. He opened the door for them when Chief McNalley identified himself and told the doctor what their business was.

Fire in their Hearts

O'Hara led them through a door at the rear of the reception area. Once inside they were met by a wall of odors of blood and cleaning solvents.

Tyler wrinkled his nose at the mix of noxious smells in the tight space. It was a good thing the fire hadn't gotten to this building, or the town would've burned for days or even weeks afterward. With all the chemical bottles he saw on the shelves lining one of the walls, the room was a firetrap waiting to happen. The place really needed a woman's touch to give it life.

Lying atop an examination table, on his back with his eyes closed, lay young Jim. His still form was lit by the glow from two oil lamps strong enough to illuminate the room. The pallor of the constable's skin made him look as if he were made of wax rather than the pinkish hue he had when they'd last seen him. Except for a plain, white, blood-stained sheet that covered him up to his waist, he was naked. The doctor had obviously removed the exterior clothing to allow him to thoroughly examine the body.

Tyler almost looked away, he found it unsettling seeing Jim lying for all intents and purposes naked on the table. But he managed to suppress his feelings. He needed all the information he could get to solve this case.

Tyler glanced at Harry, who looked paler than usual. He thought for a moment the burly blacksmith was going to be ill, until he caught Harry's eyes and the big man nodded at him with a weak smile. Tyler gave the man a slight smile of his own to reassure him. Harry nodded. *He'll be okay.*

"How did he die?" said Tyler, breaking the silence at last.

"Two bullets to the abdomen, I'd say," replied the doctor, who pulled down the sheet a small amount to reveal two black holes in the mid-section of the corpse.

174

"Large caliber by the look of them. I know this because of the blood splatter on the constable's clothing."

Tyler eyed the doctor, his eyebrows arched upward in surprise. "And what does this mean, anything?"

The doctor nodded, then moved to a small pine table set against one wall near the edge of the rings of light cast by the lamps. He came back with Jim's shirt and uniform jacket. He spread the two pieces of clothing over Jim's prone body to reveal two holes that marked the entrance of the bullets into Jim's body.

"I've been studying the reports of testimony of one Dr. William Hodgeson Ellis who testified at a rape murder case in New York City in 1863. He stated that the significance of the number, size, and position of bloodstains left on the clothes of an accused were in a pattern that was consistent with the direction of fire from the murder weapon. He called his technique, 'blood stain pattern analysis.'

"Using similar techniques, but working from the victim's direction, I managed to determine that the bullets that killed this young man were fired from close range." He paused to point at the first of the rough tears in the thick fabric of the uniform. "The dark discoloration surrounding the hole in the jacket is very likely gunpowder residue." He then pointed to the red-brown blood stains that fanned out from the hole in the fabric. "These stains suggest he was seated at the time of the fatal shots. If you stretch the fabric thus." He demonstrated by pulling the fabric flat. "You see the stains look as if they are now in strips. Blood pools on clothing, so he must've been seated."

He next lifted the white cotton shirt with more blood stains and a similar rip in the fabric where the bullets entered.

"The analysis of the blood splatter on the shirt confirms my hypothesis."

He carried the shirt and the jacket back to the table then returned to stand next to Jim's body. "I can safely conclude this man was murdered at close range before he had a chance to react. This suggests he knew his assailant, and was therefore unprepared."

Tyler glanced at Harry who shrugged. "That seems like a large leap in logic, don't you think?" said Tyler.

"No," said McNalley, his voice grim and wearing an expression to match. Only now there seemed to an underlying fire that had suddenly burst from inside him. "It's possible. In fact it's very likely true. All of it."

McNalley started for the door. "Com'on."

"Thanks, Doc," said Tyler, taking the physician's hand in his and shaking it.

The doctor nodded. "May I release the body for burial?"

"Not yet," came the echo of McNalley's voice from the lobby.

Tyler shrugged and the doctor rolled his eyes. Tyler knew that without ice the shell that once housed Jim Nelson would soon get very ripe laying here in the doctor's examination room. A corpse wasn't the best thing to have in your office when you were the only doctor in town and the locals were dependent on you for every injury or mishap.

Tyler and Harry followed McNalley into the street. The broad-shouldered chief constable was headed down the street at a quicker-than-normal gait.

Tyler ran to catch up to him. "Chief! What the hell's going on?"

Tyler caught the eye of a group of women with kids who cast disdainful looks at his choice of words. He finally managed to catch up with the chief and they strode forward like bulls headed for the nearest cow pasture in fall.

"Chief, for God's sake, what's going on?" he whispered.

"Miss Victoria is in danger," McNalley replied, his eyes focused on the task ahead. "I'm gonna get my gun and meet you and Harry at the Brighton Hotel. I just hope we're not too late."

Tyler stopped and waited for Harry. When the blacksmith caught up Tyler said, "Whoever murdered Jim is after Victoria. Let's go."

The men broke into a fast jog as they headed down streets filled with horses, wagons, and people hurrying about the town. Construction was now in full swing. They dodged the horse-drawn wagons filled with lumber, nails, saws, and hammers in the dust-choked streets.

Tyler shivered, his heart turned cold as he pictured Victoria lying on the doctor's examination table like young Jim. His pace quickened as they neared the street where the Brighton Hotel stood.

***

They arrived at the hotel to find Victoria and Emily standing on the front porch of the hotel, looks of astonishment on their faces at the sight of the two men rushing toward them. The new hotel and a few other buildings next door and across the street were the only things in this area to escape the fire.

Construction had started next to the hotel and the workmen could be seen carrying wooden beams and adding them to the partially completed building. Tyler knew that soon the new building would be complete..

Fire in their Hearts

Victoria cradled a Winchester carbine in her slim pale arms and looked down the street.

Tyler's eyes fixed on hers as he ran toward her. His heart pounded in his chest, not from exertion, but from the burning need to hold and to protect her.

Her blonde hair, capturing rays of sunlight, seemed to sparkle in the summer air. The warm breeze lifted the strands of her hair and made it look as if they were dancing around her head. It looked as if there was a halo of gold around her face. Her expression went from worry to joy as she saw him. Her smile made his heart swell in his chest.

He rushed toward her as she came down the stairs with her skirts held in her left hand, and the rifle in the other. She dropped her skirt as her left arm reached out ready to hold her love.

Suddenly, a woman's voice echoed off the half-reconstructed building next to them. It sent a chill down Tyler's spine and he felt the small hairs of his neck stand upright.

"Everyone stay right where they are if you want to keep this pretty little lady alive."

It was Rose. The one who'd kidnapped Victoria. She came around the side of the hotel and stood there as if she was waiting for everyone to notice her.

There she was, her scarlet hair spilling over her shoulders, a Winchester held out in front of her aimed at Victoria. Seeing her assailant with a rifle aimed at her, Victoria froze and her skin paled. A look of fear crossed her face as she shifted her gaze to Tyler.

With a roll of his wide shoulders, Tyler started a headlong sprint toward Victoria. Running hard, he heard Rose shout at him.

He didn't bother to acknowledge her words.

He fixed his eyes on his intended target, Victoria. The entire street was quiet.

His head was down, his arms and legs pumping furiously. He ran faster than he'd ever thought himself capable of. In seconds he was within a few feet of Victoria. His brown eyes met her blue ones as he heard the crack of a gun.

He had to get to her. He had to save her.

Tyler stretched out his arms as he came close to Victoria. He grabbed her about the waist, and covered her with his body as they fell. Any bullet intended for her would have to go through him first.

She went down with a muffled cry of pain, she hit the dirt street hard and his full weight landed on top of her.

Surprisingly, there was no sharp bite of a bullet ripping into his back as he lay atop Victoria, shielding her. He waited for a moment, rolled to one side, then jumped to his feet fully prepared to defend his lady.

Tyler looked up and stared in disbelief at the prone form of Rose; she was lying face down in the street. An expanding pool of dark red ran down both sides of her head, mingling with her long hair. She was dead.

Tyler stood next to Victoria as he looked around the street and buildings but couldn't see who had fired the shot.

He turned his gaze to Victoria's as he bent down to help her up. He needed to get her out from the open street as quickly as possible.

Tyler and Victoria wrapped their arms around each other. Their hearts seemed to beat as one as they held each other. Time seemed to slow. The world faded and narrowed to include only each other.

"How touching," said a sarcastic male voice. Tyler recognized the voice as Parson Sloan. He grimaced as he turned to face Sloan .

What now? His body felt like it was made of rubber as exhaustion set in. The tension of the past several moments had taken its toll on him. Now he'd need to pull himself together to find the stamina to fight another threat.

Tyler stood unsteadily on his feet, his breathing ragged. He raised his head as he looked at Sloan.

Tyler saw Sloan standing near the corner of one of the newly finished buildings, the rebuilt feed store. A still smoking six-gun was in his left hand and a evil grin on his narrow features. His wide-brimmed black hat was low over his eyes to shade him from the intense sunlight.

It was almost noon, Tyler could feel and smell the salty trickle of sweat run down his back.

Victoria glanced up at him, fear in her eyes. He looked down at her, he knew she feared more for him than for her own life. But he was forced to look away from her gaze to stare at the man who had the answers he sought. Only Sloan knew what this was all about. Only he knew who was behind the kidnapping. Tyler knew he needed to capture Sloan alive if he was going to find those answers.

Seventeen

AS TYLER STEPPED away from Victoria he nudged her toward the Brighton Hotel. Victoria walked backwards away from him until she reached the hotel.

Sloan moved from the side of the building until he stood in the street.

Tyler thumbed the six-gun in his holster, his dark eyes focused all the while on the man at the end of the street.

From behind him, Tyler heard footfalls as the Smarts reached Victoria and helped her up the stairs and into the lobby of the hotel. While he knew it only took a matter of seconds, it seemed to take far too long for them to all reach safety. He waited, his body tense.

Finally, he heard the hotel's front door slam and Tyler felt an sense of relief wash over him. She was safe.

The townspeople who had been going about their business disappeared when the first shots rang out on the bustling street. Now a crowd gathered along the sidewalks to watch. Others rushing to shelter in nearby buildings and gain some cover from the impending, deadly confrontation. Fear and tension were thick in the air.

Fire in their Hearts

All the while Sloan stood there in the middle of the street, his eyes cold and dead , his evil grin displayed for all to see. *He's enjoying this*. Even though he'd just killed Rose, he seemed to relish not only her death, but also in the fear he'd caused among the citizens of Vancouver.

The parson started toward Tyler, his six-gun at his side. His eyes blazed with a maniacal gleam and his face was filled with arrogance and overconfidence. His eyes were fixed on the gambler as Tyler slowly strode toward him. "Drop your gun belt, Brother Scott, or…."

"Or what?" Harry's deep voice rolled down the street. "Sick dangerous animals need to be put down, it's only right."

Tyler heard the blacksmith's voice from somewhere over his left shoulder, then the click of a hammer being drawn back.

"Harry! No! Leave him to me!" Tyler shouted, but he didn't dare look behind him to where the blacksmith stood. He couldn't take his eyes off Sloan, whose smile had faded when he heard and saw Harry. It was a momentary distraction, maybe enough to be the difference.

Tyler stopped moving then pulled his own six-gun out from its leather holster in one fluid movement and pointed it at Sloan. "Don't move, Parson. Drop your gun."

Sloan was no more than twenty feet away now and focused on Harry. His eyes went wide as he glanced at Tyler.

"Damn you, Scott. I was about to become the richest man in these parts. I'm not about to let you or anyone else steal my moment of triumph." He began to lift his gun, pointing it at Tyler.

Tyler cocked the hammer on his own revolver. "No! Don't!"

Sloan didn't listen, his eyes determined. Just as Sloan's gun came level Tyler fired.

The bullet stuck Sloan in the chest and caused him to spin to the right. He dropped to his knees facing away from Tyler. He was holding his gun loosely in his fingers now, a groan escaped his lips.

Tyler rushed toward the wounded man. He saw the six-gun slip from Sloan's grasp and drop into the street, kicking up a small cloud of brown dust. As Tyler reached him, Sloan began to sway as if he were caught in a high wind. He fell over onto his right side. Tyler caught the wounded man before he hit the street and held him with both hands around his narrow shoulders, gently laying him on his back.

Sloan was still alive, but his breaths slowed and grew more ragged. Tyler knew his lungs were filling with blood. The bubbling and gurgling sounds coming from his mouth told him that the end was near. Tyler was desperate to find out who was behind the kidnapping, he needed to work fast.

He knelt and cradled Sloan's head in his left arm holding him up off the street. Sloan looked defiantly at him while his body was weakening in Tyler's arms with each passing second.

"Sloan," Tyler said softly, "you don't have much time. If you want to clear your conscience before you go to your Maker, I'd suggest you tell me who's behind the kidnapping of Victoria McNichol."

Sloan's eyes gradually dimmed, his features paled. His heart was beating slower now toward its inevitable stop. His expression softened as the life continued to drain from his body. He motioned for Tyler to bend closer. Tyler leaned over and pressed his ear to the parson's lips. There was a whisper, then Sloan's body trembled as he took his last breath.

Tyler stared into Sloan's unseeing eyes, then upward at the blue sky.

A gull passed overhead, its mournful cry announcing to the heavens that another soul was gone.

Victoria rushed out of the hotel and knelt next to Tyler. He gently laid Sloan's body down in the street, reached out, and with gentle fingers shut his eyes.

He looked into Victoria's bright eyes filled with longing and concern. "I'm all right," he said. She smiled and nodded.

A single tear escaped her eye and traveled down her flushed cheek. Tyler lifted one finger to capture the shiny traveler.

A crowd of people gathered around them as they stood up from the dusty road.

Hank and Emily stood nearby holding hands, hanging their heads in shame. Harry stood with a calm, serious expression on his robust face. The chief constable huffed and puffed as he came toward them at a furious pace with Mayor Diller beside him looked decidedly worried.

"Mr. Scott," began McNalley, "why didn't you wait as I'd instructed before taking on this man?"

Tyler and Victoria stood as one, each with an arm around the other's waist.

"Chief, I'm sorry, but we didn't have time to get you, it all happened so fast. Parson Sloan here killed that woman." Tyler indicated the red-haired woman lying face down in the street.

McNalley's bushy eyebrows rose in surprise and Mayor Diller wrung his hands. "So many murders," said Diller, obviously beside himself. "What will people think of our town?"

"People will think we've thwarted a gang of kidnappers and saved a woman's life," said Tyler. He drew Victoria close.

Diller looked thoughtful as he rubbed his chin with chubby fingers. "Yes, of course."

He glanced at McNalley. "Chief Constable, I want this mess cleaned up immediately."

"Yes, Mr. Mayor."

Harry came up to the assembled group, a satisfied grin pasted on his features. "Well, I guess that about wraps this up, don't you think, Ty?"

Tyler shook his head. "No, Harry, not quite. I'm sorry to say, but there is one more man we have to see."

Victoria looked puzzled. "What is it, Ty?"

"Sloan told me who was behind the kidnapping and I think I know what this was all about. We have to pay a visit to Philip Walker."

Eighteen

PHILIP WALKER SAT in a brocade wingback chair in the parlor of his home, staring in horror at Tyler Scott and Victoria McNichol, who sat across from him in matching chairs. Ornate china cups filled with fragrant, hot tea sat on matching side tables next to each of them. The tea grew cooler with each passing second, mirroring the atmosphere in the room.

Tyler had just dropped a bombshell in the quiet room. The heavy silence was broken only by the rhythmic ticking of the clock on the mantle of the floor-to-ceiling fireplace.

"You're accusing *me*?" Walker voice was edged with rage, his cheeks were flushed with anger and his left hand tapped his thigh.

Tyler noticed Walker's hand tapping. *Finally a tell. He must really be shook up.*

"Before he died, Sloan told me the mastermind behind the kidnapping was from Boston. There are only two people other than yourself in this town with a connection to Boston. Victoria, and the poor, unfortunate James Nelson," said Tyler. His long fingers steepled in front of him. His elbows rested on arms of his chair. "Since Constable Nelson's dead, and Victoria certainly would not have had herself kidnapped, yes, I think you are connected.

186

"The questions now are, who in Boston is ultimately responsible and why?"

"Mr. Scott, while it's true I paid the chief constable and the mayor to get you and Victoria to leave town, I most certainly had nothing to do with those violent criminals. Victoria's father is my employer and my friend. The last thing I would want is any harm to come to his only daughter." Philip Walker eased back in his chair, his breathing measured as he visibly struggled to keep his emotions in check.

Tyler shrugged his broad shoulders as he stole a concerned glance at Victoria. Her full lips grimaced slightly then her expression became as passive as before. They'd agreed to bait Walker into revealing what he knew. It might be that he was an innocent party to the events of the past several days.

"Mr. Walker, while I don't wish to question your honor, I suspect you know more than you're telling us." Tyler looked calmly at Walker, watching for any tells. Being a professional gambler was very good training in reading another person's body language.

Walker shifted forward in his chair, his left hand smoothed his pant leg. He continued tapping his leg. His face was now a mask of purple rage. "How dare you accuse me, sir! Who in God's name do you think you are?"

"I'm a man in love, and if the woman I love is in danger I will protect her with all my being."

Walker jumped to his feet. Tyler braced himself as he prepared for a frontal assault. "That's the problem with you, Mr. Scott. You can't be in love with this woman." Walker waved one hand in Victoria's direction. "She is betrothed to another man. A man from the most powerful family in Boston."

Tyler looked at Walker. *Why have I thought that the person from Boston had to be in Vancouver?*

Walker suddenly froze, his gray eyes whirling with mixed emotion as he realized what he was saying. "Get out of my house," he said abruptly. "This conversation is over. I'll speak of this no more. I..."

"Philip! Enough!" Connie Walker entered the room, announced by the rustle of her skirts. Her black leather shoes snapped against the polished floorboards as she moved toward them. Behind her was Anna, the maid. The dark woman's eyes were averted and fixed on the floor as she entered. The maid's hands were trembling.

Connie held her head high, regally, as her calm serious eyes met her husband's. A deep frown furrowed her normally smooth brow. Her hands were clasped in front of her, her knuckles were white with the tension. She marched up to stand next to her husband, whose face had paled and whose eyes now reflected fear.

"We should have a little talk about this matter," said Connie, her voice even and controlled. She faced Victoria and calmly said, "My dear, there are some things you need to know."

Victoria nodded, looking at each one of them as she took a deep breath. "Yes, and there are things I need to tell you, as well. I'm here not just to play at the poker gathering. Father sent me to find out who has been trying to sway the Canadian Pacific Railroad and the government from building the terminus in Vancouver rather than New Westminster. I went to the surveyor's office and purchased a map of Vancouver and remembered that the terminus was going to go in at Granville and portions of that land had been marked as Crown land. But Father told me how much land they needed and that they were still short for the size of terminus they wanted to build.

188

"When I received a copy of the Incorporation documents listing the top real estate owners, I noticed Mr. Sloan had acres on Granville Street that had been traded for twice as much land in New Westminster."

"Yes, for the Canadian Pacific Railroad to come here they had to have certain properties. To get them the city traded the property on Granville for the property in New Westminster." Philip nodded, took a breath as if he was going to continue, but stopped.

Victoria looked at him and nodded. "That would make sense. I think that Sloan was betting that New Westminster would get the terminus and his property would be worth a lot of money. I wonder if he was the one sending the unfavorable reports to Ottawa?"

"As part of the Granville deal they also traded him a smaller parcel south of Terminal Avenue in Vancouver so actually he had property in both cities. He did very well on that trade. As for who was sending the reports, I suppose we'll never know," Philip said as he looked at Victoria.

"So has the official decision been made?" asked Victoria.

Philip looked at Connie and smiled. "Yes, but if I tell you it can't leave this room. There will be an official announcement and presentation next week." Philip looked around the room and they all nodded. He got up and went to the door, there was no one there, he came back and sat down. "All right then, the decision has been made that the terminus will be Vancouver."

"I'm sure that your father can find out who sent the reports now that the decision for the terminus has been made," said Tyler.

"What about you, Connie? Did you do well on your property deal as well?" asked Victoria. Her voice shook slightly.

"Yes, we did very well. The land my father-in-law, Clifford Walker, invested in was traded for one parcel in the city of Vancouver and another good size chunk in an outlying town." Connie smiled at Victoria. "I brokered the deal and the commission was very nice."

Connie started to bite her lower lip as she looked at Philip, whose eyes were as round as saucers.

"What about Philip? I understand that Philip wasn't named as one of the trustees for the Canadian Pacific Railroad. It would have been a great job for you. I was surprised and sorry to hear you didn't get it," said Victoria as she watched Connie.

"It was offered to me, but it's something I never wanted. I have no desire to work for the government and all that red tape. I like my job working with Hiram and the Canadian Pacific Railroad just fine, thank you." Philip shook his head and he looked at Connie and gave her a soft smile.

"Don't worry about us, Victoria. I wanted Philip to have the position and wrote your father, and when he answered, I found out from him that Philip didn't want the position at all." Connie's voice was clipped and short, her mouth a firm line. "We hadn't really discussed it and after I wrote to Hiram I felt foolish. I disagree with Philip, it would have been a prestigious position, but that's between us."

Connie looked at Philip who nodded, then she looked back at Victoria. Connie sat straighter in her chair and squared her shoulders.

"Now Philip and I have to let you know something else as well," Connie said as she turned to Victoria. Connie's voice was firm and clipped, a tone of voice Victoria had never heard from Connie before.

Victoria's eyes went wide with surprise. Connie had always been like her big sister. Now it was as if she'd never known her at all. The older woman looked at her as if she were an object, with no emotion at all. The hard eyes and grim determination on her face was a look that Victoria was totally unfamiliar with.

Tyler nodded and glanced at Victoria, who looked like she was in shock.

Anna left them alone with instructions to bring more tea as Connie sat in one of the remaining chairs unconsciously smoothing her dress with her slender fingers. Finally she looked up, and a soft breath escaped her lips as if she'd been holding it.

"Victoria, first of all what we did, we did for your own good," said Connie.

Victoria was silent as she watched Connie relate the heinous plot hatched by her fiancé, Hebert Littlefield, the man she was supposed to marry.

"Victoria, what I'm going to tell you is going to be very hurtful. But please let me explain everything, then we can talk about it," said Connie. She took a deep breath and calmly folded her hands on her lap and continued.

"Herbert's gambling was out of control, he had been cut off from his father's money—something he never revealed to you. He was running short of funds, so he contracted Rose Patterson, a woman he'd met in the gambling halls of San Francisco and hatched this plot. She was to kidnap you and demand a ransom. That would allow him to get his hands on your father's money before the wedding, to tide him over until you were married.

191

Fire in their Hearts

After the wedding, as Hiram McNichol's son-in-law, Herbert hoped to have unlimited access to your family's fortune to help feed his habits and maintain his lifestyle of booze, gambling, and women." Connie said as she unfolded her hands and smoothed down her skirts. There were white welts where her fingers had pressed into her hands.

"Rose?" asked Victoria in a small confused voice.

"Yes," Connie said. "Rose Patterson was one of his many lovers."

Tyler watched as Victoria turned white, it looked like she was going to be ill, instead she sat up straight and listened closely as Connie continued her story.

"I agreed to help when Sloan and Rose approached me. It was the only way to ensure your safety during the kidnapping. Rose told me that she'd make sure to highlight our willingness to help the future heir to the Littlefield fortune. I thought, at the time, that Herbert would be a powerful alley when it came to Philip's advancement and no one would have to know the truth except for us."

Connie paused and reached for her cup of tea. It rattled as it shook in her hands so she put it back on the table.

"Finish it, Connie," said Philip, his voice stern and his jaw clenched.

Connie nodded as she picked up her tea with a shaky hand again, took a sip, then continued. " It was only once the young constable was killed that I realized I was too far over my head and decided to confide in Philip. He had known nothing of the plot until just before you showed up today." Connie looked at Philip then at Victoria, tears filled her eyes. "I am so sorry."

A single tear escaped Philip's eye as his expression changed to loving concern for his wife.

"Although our union was originally more like a corporate merger than the joining of two young people, I soon came to learn I loved Philip more than life itself," Connie said. "I had hoped that one day you would feel the same for Hebert." Her head dropped and her shoulders sagged. "I know now you could never love such a man as Herbert Littlefield. I'm horrified by all the death and deception that has gone on."

Tyler looked at Victoria, "It seems that your fiancé is behind a lot of things, especially your being kidnapped."

"Oh, Connie. Herbert and Sloan were behind everything, the killings, my kidnapping, and probably the political rumors of the Canadian Pacific Railroad terminus. I wonder if they had anything to do with the actual fire, too?" Victoria looked from one face to the next.

There was a long silence as the assembled group tried to digest the tale of deceit and lies that had enveloped the lives of the four people in the parlor and the entire city of Vancouver. The clock on the mantel ticked away, marking each passing second.

"Connie, I know you thought you were doing the right thing for me. But I'm in love with Tyler." Victoria's blue eyes traveled to fix on the dark sparkling eyes of Tyler Scott. "I love him with all my heart like I've never loved another man."

"No!" said Philip firmly. "He's not to be trusted. Get rid of Littlefield, fine. I'm sure your father will help you with that. But we paid this man to get you out of town. I put up the funds personally. You cannot marry this man. He has no station. No prospects. Your father would forbid it."

193

"I don't care about any of that," said Victoria firmly. "I love him and I'm going to marry him."

Tyler broke into an easy grin. "If your referring to the partial payment I received to get her out of town, you can have it back. I only took it so I could be involved with keeping Victoria safe." He turned to Victoria. "As for marriage, I don't believe I've asked you yet, Miss McNichol."

"You will soon enough," she said with a wink.

He chuckled, the corners of his eyes crinkling at the corners. "First things first. As to my good name, you'll find that every dollar is here. I even took the horse hire and provisions out of my stake." Tyler almost chocked at that. He knew he had done the right thing, but it would leave him in a very tight position at the gather. He dug the money out of his pockets and put it in a pile in front of Philip.

Philip looked at the pile of money then at Tyler. "Keep it. I misjudged you, I'm sorry. If it weren't for you Victoria would be dead." He paused and looked at Connie. "Call it an early wedding present."

"Oh, no, it's not. This money is yours fair and square, Tyler. Besides, we can't have a wedding until we have an engagement, and so far I haven't even heard the question asked yet." Connie started to smile at both Tyler and Victoria.

"Okay, here I go." Tyler smiled at Connie and Philip. His heart was beating hard in his chest, he had never been so nervous. He rose from his chair, crossed the room, then dropped to one knee. He clasped Victoria's right hand as his gaze fixed on her dazzling blue eyes. "Miss Victoria Ann McNichol, in front of these witnesses, will you make me the happiest man in the world and marry me?"

"Yes, Mr. Tyler Scott, I will marry you," Victoria said without hesitation.

Tyler stood and held her hand as Victoria rose from her chair and sealed their betrothal with a deep kiss.

Anna let slip a small cry of delight as she stood in the doorway with a china teapot in her right hand. On her face was a wide smile.

Philip gave his maid a withering look and changed it to a smile as Anna set to refilling the tea cups and leaving the tea pot. She quietly exited the room. Victoria and Tyler remained in their tight embrace.

"It looks like there's going to be a wedding," said Connie, smiling at Tyler.

Philip nodded, scowling. "Yes, I suppose there will be. Hiram is going to have my guts for garters over this."

Connie shook her head. "Oh, no, Philip, I don't think so. Not after you tell him about Herbert and his plans."

Philip sighed heavily. "Yes, I guess that part may be all right, but she's going to marry an *American* gambler? Hiram will still have a fit."

"Look, their both gamblers, it works. As for a job, Hiram will be fine when Tyler is the stationmaster for the new railroad station here in Vancouver."

Philip looked back at his wife quizzically. "What new railroad station?"

"Why, the one you're going to have to build in Vancouver, of course," Connie said, smiling as she took a sip of her tea.

"If he's the new station master, then what am I going to be doing?"

Fire in their Hearts

"You'll be in charge of building the terminus and taking care of the Canadian Pacific Railroad between the Rockies and Vancouver. Then there's always any other expansion to the rail line that's needed in British Columbia." Connie smiled as she picked up the tea pot and refreshed everyone cup.

"Yes, of course." Philip sighed and rolled his eyes heavenward.

Before them, still locked in an embrace, were two hearts that were once lost and alone until they were brought together when their world was set aflame.

Two souls that now burned together as one with fire in their hearts.

About the Authors

Russ Crossley

An international selling author, Russ Crossley writes science fiction, fantasy, and mystery/suspense as well as their various subgenres. He has written several short stories and novels under the name R.G. Hart.

His latest science fiction satire set in the far future, *Revenge of the Lushites*, was released in the fall of 2013 and is a sequel to *Attack of the Lushites,* which was released in 2011. Both titles are available in e-book and trade paperback.

He has sold several short stories that have appeared in anthologies from various publishers, including WMG Publishing, Pocket Books, and St. Martin's Press.

He is a member of SF Canada and is past president of the Greater Vancouver Chapter of Romance Writers of America. He is also an alumnus of the Oregon Coast Professional Fiction Writers Master Class taught by award-winning author/editors Kristine Katherine Rusch and Dean Wesley Smith.

Feel free to contact him on Facebook, Twitter, or his website http:www.russcrossley.com. He loves to hear from readers.

Rita Schulz

Rita lives on the Sunshine Coast in British Columbia with Russ, her husband, who is also a fiction writer.

She has written for years and is an alumna of the Oregon Writers Network and the Greater Vancouver Chapter of the Romance Writers of America.

Her most recently published stories are *Fire in Their Hearts* with R.G. Hart from Champagne books, and *Ladies of the Jolly Roger* and *Tales of the Fantastic* from 53rd Street Publishing.

Please visit her website at http://www.ritaschulz.com to view her other works.

Selected titles from 53rd Street Publishing you may enjoy

For a more complete bibliography go to http://www.53rdstreetpublising.com

Other titles by Russ Crossley

Razor and Edge Mysteries
The Kidnapping of Billy Buttons
String of Pearls
Death by Clown
Beggin' For Murder
Ragged Ice
The Grand Central Mystery
A Strange Case of Undead Murder

Jazz Stiletto Mysteries
A Day Without Sunshine
Skullduggery
Instrument of Justice (first published in Over My Dead Body online mystery magazine)

The Amanda Dark paranormal mysteries
Hook Island
Grind Manor
Moonrise Diner
A Father's Daughter
My Partner the Zombie published in the
Hungry For Your Love Anthology (St. Martin's Press)

The Trudy Wilson Mystery Novel Series
Bad Loyalty
Shear Murder
*Buzzcut (*coming soon)

Blaster Squad Novel Series
Blaster Squad #1 Terror on the Moon
Blaster Squad #2 Sea of Death
Blaster Squad #3 Planet of Doom
Blaster Squad #4 Raiders of Cloud City
Blaster Squad #5 Dawn of the Empire (coming soon*)*

Other Novels
Attack of the Lushites
Revenge of the Lushites
My Zombie Prince
Antique Virgin
The Fire In Their Hearts with Rita Schulz
Zomopolis
The Last Serial Killer

Other titles by Rita Schulz

Short Fiction
Blarney
Flower & Bird
Party Central
Once Upon a Time

The Scarlet Curse
Spoken Words
The Brownie's Holiday
A Little Old Fashioned
In The Land of Dragons
A Little Kitchen Magic
Silver Light
For Pete's Sake
Cleaning Up is Hard to Do
Confessions of a Bold Maiden
All for One
Lucky List
A Spark of Courage
Party Line
Spoken Words

Collections
Ladies of the Jolly Roger with Russ Crossley
Ten Tempting Tales with R.S. Meger
The Fantastic Five with R.S. Meger
Unique Tales of the Fantastic
Tales of the Fantastic
Mosaic

Novels
Fire In Their Hearts with Russ Crossley
*Old Bones (*coming soon)
Tea For Two (coming soon*)*

Another exciting title by Rita Schulz coming soon from 53rd Street Publishing. Look for more details about this title soon at http://www.53rdstreetpublishing.com

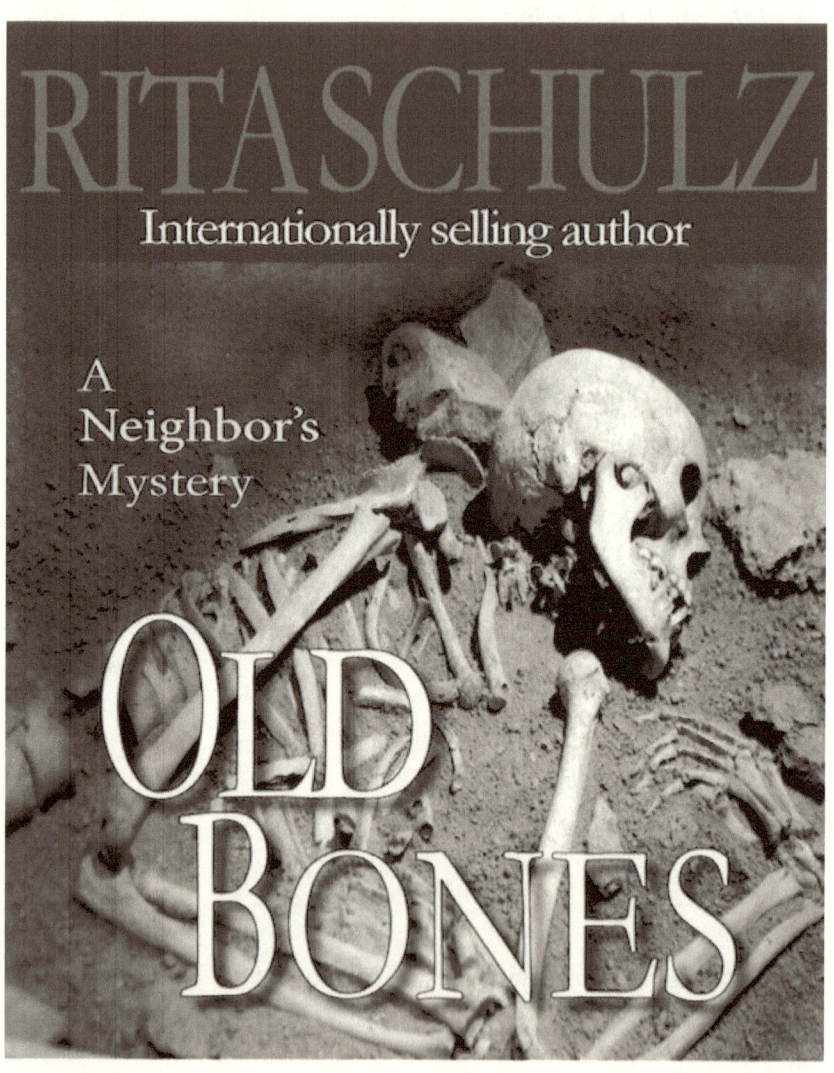

RITA SCHULZ

Internationally selling author

A Neighbor's Mystery

OLD BONES